"Gillette, Barri," Mr. Larson, the auditions director, called. Barri froze. Her heart jumped to her throat, and her feet wouldn't move. She broke out in a cold sweat.

Melanie nudged her. "Go—!"

Scrambling to her feet, Barri headed for the stage and wished she'd never agreed to audition. Ward waited while she fumbled with the script, pointing out the death scene.

The Ward McKenna. Five-nine or ten, striking blue eyes, California-tan skin, and a huge dimple creasing his right cheek. He was more handsome up close, Barry realized, hoping she didn't look as lovesick as some of the other actresses.

"I guess I don't have to worry about fouling up my lines," Ward said, as if amused, as he lay across the stage.

"Okay, let's go," Mr. Larson said. "Start with Juliet waking up. I'll be the friar."

Barri lay on the stage and tried to concentrate. Slowly, she roused herself, as if she were still half-asleep. "O comfortable friar! Where is my lord? I do remember well where I should be...." She felt herself become Juliet and saw the love of her life dead at his own hand. Speaking Shakespeare's verse, she fell to her knees, pretended to find a cup clasped in Ward McKenna's hand and when that cup was empty, she held s over Ward's mouth of excitement swept h e next words. Hopi r Romeo's death, she from Romeo and the ....ible knife in her abdomen. She fell across Ward's body, felt his muscles tense, and then lay still.

OTHER FAWCETT GIRLS ONLY TITLES:

The SISTERS series
by Jennifer Cole

THREE'S A CROWD (#1)
TOO LATE FOR LOVE (#2)
THE KISS (#3)
SECRETS AT SEVENTEEN (#4)
ALWAYS A PAIR (#5)
ON THIN ICE (#6)
STAR QUALITY (#7)
MAKING WAVES (#8)
TOO MANY COOKS (#9)
OUT OF THE WOODS (#10)
NEVER A DULL MOMENT (#11)
MOLLIE IN LOVE (#12)
COLLEGE BOUND (#13)
AND THEN THERE WERE TWO (#14)
THE BOY NEXT DOOR (#15)
CAMPUS FEVER (#16)
LOVE IS IN THE AIR (#17)
MAKING UP (#18)

The BLUE RIBBON series
by Chris St. John

RIDING HIGH (#1)
A HORSE OF HER OWN (#2)
KATE'S CHALLENGE (#3)
GOLDEN GIRL (#4)
TIME-OUT FOR JESSIE (#5)
THE MAIN EVENT (#6)

The HEARTBREAK CAFE series
by Janet Quin-Harkin

NO EXPERIENCE REQUIRED (#1)
THE MAIN ATTRACTION (#2)
AT YOUR SERVICE (#3)
CATCH OF THE DAY (#4)
LOVE TO GO (#5)
JUST DESSERTS (#6)

The SATIN SLIPPER series
by Elizabeth Bernard

TO BE A DANCER (#1)
CENTER STAGE (#2)
STARS IN HER EYES (#3)
CHANGING PARTNERS (#4)
SECOND BEST (#5)
CURTAIN CALL (#6)
TEMPTATIONS (#7)
STEPPING OUT (#8)
CHANCE TO LOVE (#9)
RISING STAR (#10)
STARTING OVER (#11)
SUMMER DANCE (#12)

The SILVER SKATES series
by Barbara J. Mumma

BREAKING THE ICE (#1)
WINNER'S WALTZ (#2)
FACE THE MUSIC (#3)
TWO TO TANGO (#4)
WORLD CLASS (#5)
ICE FOLLIES (#6)

The PERFECT 10 series
by Holly Simpson

CASEY AND THE COACH (#1)
BREAKING THE RULES (#2)
TO BE THE BEST (#3)
DREAMTIME (#4)
ONE STEP AWAY (#5)
CAMP CHAMPION (#6)

The PORTRAITS COLLECTION®

SUMMER HEAT (#1)
ATTITUDES (#2)
STEALING JOSH (#3)
ALWAYS (#4)
THE UNCERTAINTY PRINCIPLE (#5)
BETWEEN FRIENDS (#6)

STAR STRUCK

CENTER STAGE #1

ELLEN ASHLEY

FAWCETT GIRLS ONLY • NEW YORK

CHAPTER ONE

"DON'T you tell a soul!" Barri Gillette whispered to Felicia, her fat tabby cat.

Unconcerned about Barri's soon-to-be-launched acting career, Felicia went about washing her face. The yellow cat was curled up on the tufted pillow at the vanity in Barri's bedroom, sunning herself near the window, oblivious to the posters of stage and movie stars tacked to every available space on the walls and ceiling.

"Yeah, a lot you care," Barri said with a wry smile. She licked the edge of the envelope, then taped it for good measure. "I'm on my way to stardom, and this"—she waved the envelope in front of Felicia's pink nose—"is my ticket!"

Felicia yawned.

"Great," Barri muttered, glancing down at the envelope again, making sure that the address for the television studio in New York was correct. She tugged open her desk drawer, rummaging through its contents and tossing aside old movie magazines, ticket stubs, and reviews of her favorite plays.

"What're you looking for?"

Barri froze, then glanced over her shoulder.

Her eight-year-old brother, Jeff, Little League pitching star for Los Tacos Locos, was leaning against the frame of her open door. As always, his navy blue cap was perched cockeyed on his head, and his unkempt light brown hair poked out from beneath the bill.

Nonchalantly tossing a beat-up leather baseball in the air and catching it deftly, Jeff made a quick survey of her room.

Barri gulped and casually placed her hand over the envelope, hoping Jeff wouldn't notice. If Mom or Dad got wind of the fact that she was entering a contest for a cameo spot on "Tomorrow Is Another Day," the daytime drama in which her Aunt Laura starred, they'd flip. And Jeff was lousy at keeping secrets. "I was just looking for a stamp."

"What for?"

"Because I need one," she said, hiding the envelope in her purse. She ran a comb through her short dark curls, added a dab of mousse, then touched her lips with gloss. Her brown eyes sparkled with her secret—a chance for a part on a real television show. Sure, it was just a couple of shots, but maybe, if she was good enough, the part could be expanded into a recurring role. Then her career would soar, and she could make the jump to prime time and then movies. . . . Jeff dropped the ball. It thudded against the floor and brought Barri crashing back to the present.

"If you don't mind," she said, "I've got to get ready." She straightened her oversize peach T-shirt, grabbed her book bag, and snagged her jean jacket from her closet. Her outfit was a replica of Danielle Thomas's, a teen star of "Tomorrow Is Another Day." Barri believed she should look the part of a famous soap opera actress if she were ever going to be one. "Aren't you late for school?"

"Nah—teachers' conference or somethin'."

"The third week of school?"

He shrugged, eyeing her suspiciously. "Who're you writing to?"

"I'm not *writing* to anyone."

"Then why do you need a stamp?"

"What do you care? Where are my shoes?" She spied the toe of one white sandal poking out from beneath an unruly stack of movie magazines on her desk.

"You're acting funny." Jeff just wouldn't leave her alone.

"I am not!"

He wrinkled his freckled nose and grinned, exposing two uneven front teeth. "It's a love letter! That's what it is!"

"It's not—"

"Sure it is. You're writing a love letter to Rich!"

At that moment Barri wanted to throttle Jeff. He could be such a pain. "It's not a love letter to Rich or anyone else!" she snapped, thinking fleetingly of her boyfriend, Rich Davis. Though she really liked Rich a lot and sometimes thought she was in love with him, she couldn't imagine writing love letters to the goalie of the Fillmore High soccer team.

"Then what?" Jeff prodded.

She slung the strap of her purse over her shoulder and slid into the thong. "Out of my room," she insisted, shepherding him into the hallway just as she spotted the other sandal on the floor near her vanity. "You, too, come on! Out!" she called to Felicia as she slipped into the other shoe. Reluctantly the cat hopped off her stool, then trotted into the hall. Barri closed the door firmly behind her and said to her brother, "You may not have school today, but I do."

"Okay," he said with a grudging shrug. "It's no big deal."

"Right." At the top of the stairs she turned and wagged a finger at him. "And my room's off limits—remember?"

"Sure." He began tossing his ball again.

"Barbara!" her mother called from the kitchen. Barri hurried downstairs, her fingers trailing along the smooth wood banister. The varnish had been sanded off, and only the bare oak remained. The stairs, along with the den and extra bedroom, were the most recent of her mother's projects. An interior decorator by trade, Celia Gillette was putting her talents to work on the Gillette home, an "historic" colonial house that, in Celia's opinion, needed a top-to-bottom refurbishing.

"I thought you were going to try and remember to call me Barri," Barri reminded her mother as she entered the kitchen.

Celia Gillette, wearing a fuchsia jogging suit and matching sweatband to keep her hair off her face, rolled her eyes toward the ceiling and grinned. In Barri's opinion, her mother hardly looked forty-two. "I know, I know," Mrs. Gillette said patiently. "It's just hard to change the habits of nearly sixteen years. Besides, Barbara's a pretty name."

"It's okay, but I need something more . . . glamorous."

"I'll remember that when I see your name in lights," her mother replied with a wink. The timer buzzed loudly. Mrs. Gillette grabbed a potholder, then pulled two loaves of hot cranberry bread from the oven. "Melanie called while you were in the shower. She said she'd pick you up after she stops at Joel's house."

"Great." Barri snatched an apple from the fruit bowl and a dog-eared copy of her favorite screenplay before heading for the door.

"That's not enough breakfast! There's cinnamon toast—"

"I can't, I'm late!" Barri called over her shoulder as she dashed out the front door. Outside, the air was crisp and clear. Clouds drifted high overhead, partially obscuring a lazy autumn sun. Leaves, dry and brittle, rustled in the wind.

Barri stuffed her hands in her pockets, and she shivered but not from the cold. She was excited. She thought about the contest and crossed her fingers. She had to win—she just *had* to!

As she shrugged into her jacket, she saw Melanie Todd's silver Mustang nosing slowly around the corner of Sycamore Street. Melanie, a tall, willowy blonde who, in Barri's opinion, resembled Meryl Streep, was Barri's best friend.

Barri waved. Melanie pulled into the driveway, but Barri could hardly see her. Hunched down low, her golden crown barely visible through the windows, Melanie motioned frantically. "Get in, we're late!"

Barri opened the passenger door and slid inside. "What's going on?"

"Nothing." Peering cautiously over her shoulder Melanie backed out of the drive.

"I don't get it. Why're you—"

"It's because she ripped a contact lens," Joel Amberson announced from the back seat. Dressed in his usual outfit of worn jeans, a black T-shirt, sunglasses, and a faded green army jacket, Joel grinned. "Believe me, she thinks it's a fate worse than death."

"*It is!*" Melanie insisted.

For the first time Barri noticed Melanie's glasses. Thick lenses framed in tortoiseshell were perched on the tip of Melanie's regal nose.

"They don't look bad."

"Just horrible!" Melanie cried.

"I think they make you look intellectual," Joel mocked.

"I don't want to look like a bookworm. I want to look like a model or an actress—"

"You do!" Barri insisted.

Melanie sighed. "I don't get my new lens until Thursday!" The car lurched, sliding a little as Melanie took a corner too fast.

"Hey, watch it," Joel yelled. "Don't you know you have the next Neil Simon back here?"

"Sorry." Melanie eased up on the throttle and switched on the radio. The quick beat of a Debbie Gibson tune filled the interior. "I'll just *die* before I get my contacts back! Tryouts are Wednesday night!"

"Don't remind me," Barri said.

Joel leaned forward, placing his head squarely between Barri and Melanie. "I've been trying to tell Mel here that it won't matter if she wears her contacts, glasses, or stumbles around the stage in a myopic blur. All she has to do is convince Brookbank that she can handle the part of Jamie."

"The trouble is, Jamie isn't blind," Melanie grumbled. Barri smothered a smile. "Maybe Joel could rewrite the part."

Joel, who took his art seriously, and who wrote most of the scripts for any original production at Fillmore, including his current *Thin Ice*, lifted his shades and sent Barri a withering glance. "I never rewrite," he said disdainfully.

"Sure," Barri teased. Joel was famous with the drama club for his on-the-spot rewrites.

Snapping his glasses back onto his nose, he added, "Melanie will just have to mold herself into the part."

"Give me a break," Barri whispered.

Melanie frowned. "It won't be that easy. Ms. Brookbank has been on my case ever since I got laryngitis on opening night last spring!"

Barri smiled. "I think she's forgiven you."

"I wish." Melanie sighed as she cranked on the wheel and the Mustang rounded the final corner. Ahead, at the end of the street, stood Fillmore High.

Whenever Barri drove down this street, approaching the building head-on, she was struck by how impressive the school looked—how steeped in history. The school was a massive brick, two-storied structure designed in a traditional Ivy League style. A broad pillared porch covered the main entrance, narrow-paned windows were cut into the intricate brickwork, and vines climbed one wall.

Melanie maneuvered her sports car through a narrow alley leading to the student parking lot at the back of the building. There Barri saw the recent additions to Fillmore, two low-slung concrete wings and a new gymnasium.

"Oh, no," Melanie moaned as she pulled into the lot and noticed the throng of students gathered on the back steps. "Everyone's here!"

"Of course everyone's here, silly. The first bell hasn't rung yet!" Barri said.

"Maybe I should wait in the car."

"That's crazy."

"Come on, come on, let's get going," Joel said, pushing against Barri's seat with his knee. "My back's killing me."

Barri slid out of the Mustang.

With a melodramatic glance at Melanie, Joel unfolded his five-foot-ten-inch body from the cramped interior. "Why doesn't this woman buy a larger car for her friends?"

Melanie yanked her glasses off her nose, dumped them into her purse, then tossed her blond hair haughtily over one shoulder. "Because, smart guy, *this woman* is broke."

"You?" Barri asked, stunned. Melanie's family was well-off, her allowance for one week was more than Barri's was for an entire month. "My dad's on a new frugality kick," Melanie said with a pout. "Believe me, it's *no fun!*"

"Barri! Melanie! Over here!" Geraldine Horowitz, her long black hair streaming behind her, sprinted down the steps. She nearly slipped as the heel of her boot caught on the step, but she caught herself and rushed forward. Her face was flushed, her blue eyes bright with excitement, and she was frantically waving an orange piece of paper in the air. "You'll never guess what's going on! It's absolutely the greatest thing that's ever happened in Merion, Connecticut!" Breathless, Geraldine shoved the flyer under Barri's nose.

"What're you talking about?" Joel asked, reading over Barri's shoulder.

Barri's heart began to pound wildly. "It says that the local theater is producing *Romeo and Juliet!* And listen, there will be an open audition for all of the parts except for the part of Romeo, which will be played by Ward McKenna!"

"Ward McKenna?" Melanie squealed. "He's coming back to Merion?"

"Great," Joel muttered, obviously unimpressed.

"You have a problem with that?" Geraldine asked.

"McKenna's okay. But Romeo's a wimp!" Joel said, his lips twisting a little. "He runs around moaning after one woman, and then he starts the same routine with Juliet." He shrugged his shoulders. "I don't get what all the fuss is about."

Geraldine bristled a little. "The fuss is about Ward McKenna, that's what!"

"And I thought you were talking about Shakespeare," Joel taunted.

"Just think—*Romeo and Juliet*, here. With Ward McKenna."

Melanie sighed. "This is the perfect part for a classical actress. . . . "

Barri didn't hear much of the surrounding conversation because she was immersed in reading the announcement. To think that Ward McKenna was returning to Merion! It was almost too good to be true. She'd never met him, of course, but she'd heard all about him, especially from her older sister Kelly, who had gone to school with Ward.

He was already a Merion legend, the epitome of "local boy makes good." Handsome and tall, with jet-black hair and startling blue eyes, Ward had appeared in various productions at Fillmore. He'd moved to Los Angeles after graduation and several months later had landed a part on a prime-time television show, "Three for Breakfast," a situation comedy about three teenage brothers trying to make it on their own.

Melanie snatched the flyer out of Barri's hands, pulled it close to her nose and read, her mouth dropping open. "Is this for real?"

"Uh-huh!" Geraldine said. "I called the theater this morning and talked to the stage manager. It's true. The play will run for three weeks while Ward is on hiatus from his television show." She leaned closer and pulled out a tattered magazine from her huge black bag. "You know why he's doing it, don't you? I read about it in *Teen Idols*. He's been criticized for not being a serious actor. Some people think he got the part in 'Three for Breakfast' only because of his looks, and now he wants to make the jump to movies. So, he'll do a local production here, just to get the feel of working on the stage again, like when he did it in high school. Then I'll bet he tries to do something on- or off-Broadway to prove he can handle stage and the big screen!"

"You really read this rag?" Joel asked, appalled. He snatched the magazine from Geraldine's hand.

Geraldine ignored him. "I even asked the stage manager if he might need any help with costumes or set design, and he told me to come in and talk to him! Can you imagine!"

"No," Joel remarked dryly, thumbing through the well-worn pages of the latest copy of *Teen Idols*.

"What I wouldn't do to play Juliet!" Melanie sighed dreamily just as the bell sounded.

Me, too, Barri thought. Shouldering open the door, she could barely look at her friend. She knew that Melanie wanted the part of Juliet more than anything. Melanie considered herself a classical actress and probably wouldn't lower herself to enter a contest for a chance to be cast as an extra in a soap opera. And Barri always played lighter roles, her comic timing her greatest asset. But that didn't mean she couldn't play Juliet. She just *couldn't* pass up the opportunity to work with Ward McKenna. Even if it meant auditioning against her best friend. She grinned as she twirled the combination of her locker. Two opportunities in one day. First the contest opportunity she'd found in her most recent copy of *Soap World,* and now a chance to audition with Ward McKenna. Yes, she thought, winking at the poster of Michael J. Fox taped to the inside of her locker door, I'm on my way!

CHAPTER
TWO

THE lunchroom buzzed with the news. Everyone seemed to be talking about Ward McKenna's return to Merion. Barri set her tray on the table and slid onto the bench next to Robert Bradbury, one of her closest friends and the first person she'd met when she joined the Thespians, Fillmore High's drama club, nearly two years before.

A likable, easygoing guy, Robert was whip thin and only a couple of inches taller than Barri's five feet four inches. His wheat-blond hair was unruly, his skin perpetually tanned from skiing, and his teeth flashed in a slightly off-center smile. Mainly known at Fillmore for his technical skills with the lighting and tricky acoustics of Fillmore's theatre, he was also a great actor.

He glanced up at Barri and motioned to the cafeteria walls, where orange flyers, duplicates of the one Geraldine had been waving frantically on the school steps that morning, were taped. "I guess you heard the news."

"I couldn't have avoided it if I wanted to," she

said with a dimpled grin. "Everyone's talking about the play!"

"You mean about Ward McKenna."

"Who?" she asked, and they both laughed.

"Are you going to try out?"

"What kind of a question is that?" Geraldine scooted onto the bench next to Barri and plopped her huge bag between them. "Of course she is! Everyone at Fillmore will!"

"Everyone but Joel," Barri said.

"What's his problem anyway?" Geraldine asked, her dark brows drawing together. An exotic-looking girl to begin with, she was wearing a long black skirt, bright pink blouse, and a wild Indian batik scarf. Blue enamel earrings matched the barrettes holding her black hair away from her face. "Joel's been in a bad mood ever since he saw the flyer."

"Don't you know why?" Robert asked. "Have you even looked at the dates? The *Romeo and Juliet* thing is gonna run the week after his play here at school."

"So?" Geraldine asked.

Barri was beginning to understand. Joel had worked for six months on the script for *Thin Ice*. Joel felt, and the Thespians' advisers agreed, that *Thin Ice* was his best script—maybe even the best original play ever to be staged at Fillmore High.

"Think about it," Robert insisted as Melanie joined the table. "Everyone will be trying out for *Romeo and Juliet*, and a lot of kids will get parts, even if they're small. Who does that leave for Joel's play?"

"The rest of the school," Geraldine said.

"Yeah, but how many of them will have any experience?" He glanced around the table. "All the Thespians, plus everyone else in town will be trying out for *Romeo and Juliet*. Do you think they'll bother with an *amateur* production?"

"Maybe," Barri said, but in her heart she knew Robert was right.

"And once it's staged—who will come?"

"Everyone."

"No way. I bet the only people who show up are the parents of the kids in the play. No one will even care about *Thin Ice*."

"You don't know that," Barri said.

"Don't I? I'm one of Joel's best friends, but I'm trying out for the part of Mercutio in *Romeo and Juliet*. If I don't get the part, I'll volunteer to work with the lighting crew." He shrugged and turned back to his hamburger.

Barri's appetite died.

Geraldine said, "That's the way it is in the real world." But Barri noticed that Geraldine's normally voracious appetite had disappeared, too. She barely picked at her salad.

Barri felt a stab of guilt. If given the chance, she, too, would rather play Juliet opposite Ward McKenna than the lead in *Thin Ice*. Frowning, she swirled her straw in her drink and told herself that she had to try out for Juliet. She had to.

Barri was nearly finished toying with her lunch when Joel flopped onto the bench across from her. He was with Kurt Motulsky, another Thespian. Kurt, a singer, dancer, and musician was into music in a big way. He was wearing his Walkman, his head bobbing to a beat only he could hear.

"Move over a little," he shouted to Joel, who grudgingly slid down the bench.

Joel's features were drawn into a scowl, and he attacked his cheeseburger without a word to anyone at the table.

"Are you okay?" Barri finally asked, trying to ignore the feeling that she should have changed her name from Barbara to Benedict Arnold.

"Just great," he said. "Why wouldn't I be?"

"Because of the play."

Joel polished off his burger. "It's no big deal," he said testily. "There're plenty of actors, lighting people, set designers." His gaze swung around the table before landing back on Barri. "What're you going to do? Try out for Juliet?"

"I—I haven't really decided."

"Well, you'd better figure it out, and soon. The tryouts for *Thin Ice* are Wednesday. Since the auditions for *Romeo and Juliet* aren't until next week, we'll see who's really interested in doing what." With that he picked up his tray and walked briskly out of the room.

"He's really bent," Robert said, watching him. Barri felt her teeth sink into her lower lip. Joel was one of her best friends. She didn't want to hurt him. But she couldn't give up a chance to work with Ward McKenna. Or could she?

"Don't worry about it," Rich said later. Comfortably slinging his arm across her shoulders, Rich walked Barri back to her locker. "Joel's just moody."

"Temperamental," Barri corrected.

Rich glanced down and slanted her an amused grin. His dark eyes twinkled. "Right. He's an artist—or is it *artiste*?"

"Whichever," she said, but couldn't keep an edge to her voice. Even though she thought she should defend Joel, Barri relaxed a little and smiled. Rich had a way of making her see things in a different light. Maybe it was because he was an athlete—a jock as opposed to an artist—but whatever his special glimmer of insight was, Barri was grateful for it.

They wended their way through the crowded hallways and heard the excited chatter, all of which centered around Ward McKenna.

"I heard he's coming back to marry his hometown girlfriend!" one big-eyed freshman whispered.

"No, that's not it at all! He got kicked off the set of 'Three for Breakfast.' Something about salary demands," her friend disagreed.

"Maybe he just wanted a break," one rangy, red-haired boy speculated.

"Oh, sure, from the California sun, the beach, the girls," his friend replied, clapping the redhead between the shoulders. "Get real. Who'd want a break from *that*?"

Barri smiled to herself. No matter what the reasons for his return, Ward McKenna had certainly caused a stir at Fillmore High.

Propping one shoulder against her locker, Rich surveyed the crowded corridor. "If you ask me, this is a lot of hoopla over nothing."

"I think the phrase is *much ado about nothing.*"

Rich chuckled. "Whatever."

"Well, it's not *nothing*, believe me."

"I guess not. But look at them." He motioned toward the kids gathered in the halls. "No one seems to remember that the team could make it to state this year."

"We remember," Barri protested, poking him playfully on the chest. "But you guys aren't there yet, are you?"

His arms surrounded her waist and one corner of his mouth lifted. His brown eyes darkened a shade.

Barri felt warm inside, the way she always did when Rich hugged her.

"Maybe I'd try harder if you were a cheer-leader," he teased. She laughed and tossed him a knowing look. "You don't even hear the cheer-leaders when you're out there. You told me. Besides, I'm not cut out for pom-poms and all that rah-rah stuff."

"Okay, okay. Enough already," he said, lifting his palms in mock surrender. "It's just that I'd like you at all the games—even when the team travels."

"I'll try this year. I promise."

"Between rehearsals."

"Right. Just like you'll catch my performances between games!"

The bell clanged. Kids scattered. Rich cocked his head toward the science wing. "I'll see ya later. I can't be late for physics again. One more late slip this term and it's"—he ran one finger slowly across his throat—"curtains. Mr. Jenkins would love to see me get cut from the team."

"No way. You're too valuable."

Rich grinned. "I knew there was a reason I liked you."

"Get out of here." He took off at a trot and Barri, her book bag slung over one shoulder, headed for the library on the second floor. She half ran past the school office but stopped short when she saw the mail drop. *The contest!* With all the excitement of the day she'd forgotten to mail her entry to the television studio in New York. Cringing as the second bell rang, she scrounged in her purse, found the envelope and, crossing her fingers, dropped it into the mail slot. Maybe, with a lot of luck and some hard work, she might just be able to land the part of Juliet and win the chance to audition for the small role in "Tomorrow Is Another Day"!

"I'm sorry, every copy is checked out," the librarian told her.

"But how can that be? You have millions." Barri scanned the shelves where all of the books on Shakespeare and his plays were usually kept. An entire section had been wiped out.

"Not quite millions. It seems that there's been a sudden interest in Shakespeare today—or at least in Juliet. You might be able to get a copy of *Romeo and Juliet* from the town library. Or talk to Ms. Brookbank and Mr. Heifetz in the drama department. They must have copies of their own. Maybe they'll loan you one."

"I will. Thanks," Barri said glumly. It seemed that the entire school had been taken over by *Romeo and Juliet* fever!

She shoved open the library door and nearly collided with Melanie. "Oh—sorry," she said automatically.

Melanie waved off her apology. "It's not your fault," she admitted, reaching into her purse and slipping on her glasses. She glanced self-consciously down the empty hall. "I've been stumbling over people and walls and desks all day."

Barri spied a thick volume of Shakespeare's works tucked under Melanie's arm. "Hey, where'd you get that?"

"I got lucky. This was the last copy in the library."

Barri sighed. "I know."

"So—why don't you rehearse with me?"

"Are you kidding? I'd love it!" Barri exclaimed, brightening.

"Good—tomorrow after school?" Melanie asked. They were walking toward the art department.

"Tomorrow the Thespians meet," Barri reminded her. "We're supposed to clean up the stage for auditions on Wednesday."

"Oh, right." Melanie didn't meet her eyes. "Are— are you still trying out?" she asked. "For *Thin Ice*, I mean."

"Aren't you?"

"I don't know," Melanie admitted. "I want the part of Jamie—it's great. And I don't want to hurt Joel's feelings, but ... well, what if I get the part and then, next week, when I audition for Juliet and get it, what then?"

Barri's temper flared. "Look on the bright side— maybe you won't get the part of Jamie!"

Melanie arched one thin eyebrow. "That's negative thinking, Barri. I only think positively."

"Then maybe you should think positively about Joel's play."

"Like you?" Melanie shot back. "Are you trying out Wednesday night?"

"I don't know," Barri admitted miserably.

Melanie's lips compressed. "Maybe one of us should go out for Joel's play and one for *Romeo and Juliet.*"

"Do what?"

"Well, you know, you go out for Jamie, and I'll try for Juliet."

Barri stopped dead in her tracks. "You're kidding, right?"

"Of course not."

"I—I don't think that would work."

"Well, I don't know what else to do!" Melanie snapped, her color rising suddenly. "You know I've always considered myself a classical actress. Juliet would be perfect for me! Perfect! I—I just can't let an opportunity like this slip by. If Joel gets hurt, then he gets hurt. It's just too bad! Geraldine was right, you know. That's life!" Everything came out in a rush; then she stripped the glasses from her nose and pursed her lips.

"Look, Mel—"

"Hey, I'm sorry." Melanie rubbed her temple, as if she were trying to get rid of a headache. "I—I didn't mean to get mad. It's just that I don't understand why all this has to happen at once. The part of Juliet is a chance of a lifetime, and Joel—well, he'll write other plays."

"But this is his best."

"So try out for it."

"I—I'm going to," Barri said without really thinking.

"Good!" Melanie brightened. "Look, I'll meet you after school."

"Okay. We can talk about *Thin Ice* then."

Melanie shook her head. Her blond hair swept across her collar. "There's no reason to. I've already made up my mind, Barri. I won't give up a chance to work with Ward McKenna," she said, "not even for Joel. This is too important."

Then, as if embarrassed at her own words, Melanie whirled and headed down the hall in the opposite direction, the heels of her suede boots clicking loudly against the tiles.

Barri leaned one shoulder against the wall. She wanted to try out for the part of Juliet so badly, she could almost taste it, and yet, she didn't want to hurt Joel.

Of course there was the chance that she wouldn't get the part in *Thin Ice*. In fact, she could intentionally mess up—blow her lines. Unfortunately

Joel and Ms. Brookbank would probably see right through that charade.

"Face it, Gillette," she told herself angrily, "You're caught between the proverbial rock and a hard spot!" Or, more likely, she was skating on *thin ice.*

CHAPTER
THREE

BROOMS swished across the stage of Fillmore High's auditorium. Caught in the illumination of the stage lights, dust motes sparkled and danced.

Beyond the apron of the stage, rows of seats, now empty, stood in attendance, separated by two carpeted aisles and sloping steadily upward. A curved balcony, over which huge chandeliers hung, stretched above the exits.

To Barri the auditorium seemed gloomy. Though the houselights were up, without an audience—or a rehearsal in progress—the auditorium had all the warmth of a cave. Only a few students were working feverishly to clean the stage and organize the prop and costume rooms that were located behind the small orchestra pit.

But the following evening, during the auditions for *Thin Ice*, the auditorium would be transformed.

Already nervous, Barri could feel her stomach knotting, just thinking about auditions. What if no one showed up? Joel was already in a bad mood. How would he feel if he couldn't even cast *Thin Ice*? As she shoved a huge refrigerator box toward the back of the stage, she nearly stumbled over a plastic coat of arms, a prop that had been left from last spring's production.

"Hey—don't get rid of the carton!" Geraldine called from upstage. She'd been sweeping the apron, but let her broom drop. The wooden handle fell to the floor with a clatter. "I'll use it for the next set—"

"You mean for *Thin Ice*?" Barri asked hopefully. "You'll work on the scenery and the costumes?"

Geraldine frowned. "I don't know."

With a sigh Barri tugged on the cardboard carton. "So where do you want this monstrosity?"

"How about over there?" Geraldine pointed to the right wing. "I'll help." Together they maneuvered the box into position. "That should do it!" Geraldine, rubbing her dusty palms on her denim miniskirt, eyed the box and nodded her approval. "With a little imagination and some paint, this could be turned into just about anything."

"If you say so," Barri agreed.

Geraldine glanced at her friend. "What's wrong with you?" she asked. "You look like you just lost your best friend."

"Not my *best* one," Barri said, "but I'm worried about Joel."

"Aren't we all?" For nearly two days Joel had barely spoken a word to anyone. The rest of the Thespians, Barri included, had been walking on eggshells around him—feeling guilty and whispering about *Romeo and Juliet* behind his back.

Barri felt awful. Guilt pricked at her conscience. For the past day and a half she'd thought about the upcoming productions. One minute she'd decide to go out for both parts; the next she planned just to try out for *Thin Ice*. She'd changed her mind so many times, she wasn't sure what to do.

"Okay, everyone," Mr. Heifetz's voice boomed from backstage. "That's it for now. Let's have a quick meeting and call it a day."

Robert hurried by, picking up the plastic shield and a few other "weapons" that had been left to collect dust. "I'll put these in the prop room and be with you in a minute," he said as Geraldine and Barri clambered down the short flight of stairs from the stage. The two girls dropped into seats in the first row. They were joined by the rest of the Thespians, who sat in the remaining front-row-center seats. Only Joel, dark aviator sunglasses hiding his eyes, sat apart from the rest of the group.

"Boy, he's really rubbing it in," Melanie whispered to Barri.

"It's got to be hard." Barri whispered back.

"Well, he doesn't have to be a martyr about it."

"Shh!" Barri whispered, afraid Joel might overhear.

"Okay, people, listen up," Mr. Heifetz said as he swung himself onto the stage and faced the group. A short, lean man in his mid-thirties, with frizzy hair, oval wire-rimmed glasses, and a face that could change expression in a flash, he was dressed in black slacks, black turtleneck, and matching shoes and socks. "Tomorrow night we're holding auditions for *Thin Ice*. I hope you'll all be here. Joel's going to help direct, and he'll also be the stage manager during prerehearsal."

He paused. No one said anything. Frowning slightly, Mr. Heifetz continued, "I've asked vocational ed to help us out with the technical things. Mr. James's woodworking and drafting classes will help design and build the set, and we can count on Mrs. Pederson's home ec class to alter costumes, but you"—he looked directly at Geraldine—"will be in charge of makeup and wardrobe."

Geraldine swallowed hard. "I—I might have a little bit of a conflict," she admitted. Mr. Heifetz raised one of his bushy eyebrows. Geraldine plunged on. "I talked to the stage manager at the theater downtown. He asked me to help out during the production of *Romeo and Juliet*."

Barri squinched lower in her seat, wishing to drop right through the floor. Here it comes, she thought, inwardly flinching. From the corner of her eye, she saw Joel, his jaw set, one shoulder turned, in effect ostracizing himself from the rest of the Thespians.

Mr. Heifetz pursed his thin lips together thoughtfully. "I wondered about that," he said with a sigh. "The timing's not great."

"Not great?" Kurt grumbled. "It's awful!"

"Yeah, right. It's awful," Mr. Heifetz agreed. "But we're locked into our schedule, and so is the downtown theater. So we're stuck. Some of you will have to make choices—others will have to juggle the work. We have a commitment to the school and our productions here, but I'd be the last one to stand in your way—*Romeo and Juliet* is a classic."

Barri could almost feel Melanie's mood improve. "See," she whispered.

"However," Mr. Heifetz continued, "I think that *Thin Ice* is great—probably the best play we've ever put on here at Fillmore. It's a tough choice, but one you'll face when you're in the real world— if you're lucky. Now, any questions?" He scanned the room.

They all started reaching for their jackets and book bags.

"Okay." Mr. Heifetz clapped his hands as a signal that the impromptu meeting was over. "Be here tomorrow at six forty-five. Auditions start at seven."

Joel was out of the auditorium first. Barri snatched her books and coat and ran after him, but the door swung shut in her face. Suddenly angry, Barri shoved open the door and ran down the hall to catch up with him. "Hey—wait! Joel!"

He spun around and stood rigid, lips drawn tight, eyes hidden beneath his shades. "What?"

"I—I just wanted to walk with you. I know this is hard."

He shrugged. "No big deal."

He was lying, hiding inside himself. Barri recognized the symptoms. "Look, maybe we could go down to The Fifties and grab a soda," she suggested.

"I don't need to be humored."

"I just thought we could talk—"

"I can't. I'm late," he said.

"Late for what?"

His brows drew down over the tops of his sunglasses. "The rest of my life." Without another word he turned on his heel and shoved his shoulder into the door leading outside. It flew open and Joel, army jacket tails flapping, sprinted across the parking lot.

Barri wanted to throttle him. What a crummy thing to say! Even though he was obviously upset, he didn't have a right to take it out on her.

"A real fun guy, huh?" Geraldine said as she came up behind Barri.

"You heard?"

"The tail end of it." She shoved her dark hair over her shoulder and watched Joel round a far corner. "He can be a real pain in the rear."

"Maybe that's why he's so brilliant."

"Brilliant, schmilliant—sometimes Joel's just a jerk."

"Yeah, sometimes," Barri had to agree, but she couldn't help feeling Joel was in a black mood because he felt all his friends were turning their backs on him. She'd known Joel all his life, even before his parents had broken up when he was eleven. Since then, he'd been moodier than ever.

"Hey—wait up!" Melanie caught up with them. "Need a ride home?" she asked Barri.

"Uh-huh."

"I'll see you later," Geraldine said, ignoring Melanie and heading down the hall.

"Don't tell me she's in one of her moods, too," Melanie said, pouting a little.

"She's okay." Barri wasn't interested in getting caught in the middle between Melanie and Geraldine. She wished they liked each other better, but there wasn't much she could do about it.

"If you say so." Melanie watched Geraldine disappear around a bank of lockers. Then she turned her attention back to Barri. "Did I tell you, I picked out the scene I'm going to do for *Romeo and Juliet*—the balcony scene. What do you think?"

"The what? Oh, great," Barri murmured, though she was still thinking of Joel.

"So, what am I gonna do?" Barri groaned, sipping lemonade on the back porch and watching as her mother watered a huge terra cotta planter overflowing with scarlet-blossomed impatiens. Sighing, Barri ruffled through the pages of *Cats*, one of her favorite Broadway plays.

She couldn't concentrate on the script, no matter how hard she tried. Not today.

"It's your decision," Mrs. Gillette said. She tucked a stray strand of dark hair into her ponytail, then plucked off the dead flowers of a few straggly plants. "Joel's your friend. You say his play is good; then support him."

"And what about Juliet?"

Her mother smothered a smile. "Seems to me, she's gotten along okay without you for a few hundred years already—"

"Mom, be serious. This is my career! My life!"

"I know, I know. And far be it for me to interfere with your career, but it seems to me that friendship's worth something here."

"Joel isn't being such a great friend."

"Isn't he? I wonder why? It couldn't be because he feels abandoned, could it?"

"Oh, you don't understand!" Barri blurted out, setting her empty glass onto the table and glowering. "Joel is so ... so ... irrational sometimes. And it's all because of Mr. Heifetz!"

Her mother didn't say anything, but Barri could tell she was listening.

"He thinks Joel is something special."

"And you don't?"

"Yes! Of course he is! But so are Melanie and Kurt and the rest of the kids! Sure, Joel's talented, but ..." Barri let her voice trail off. It was hard to put into words. "But it's different with Heifetz. He was a playwright, too, and so he and Joel kind of have this writing thing in common, you know."

Mrs. Gillette straightened. "Mr. Heifetz was a playwright? What were some of his plays?"

Barri shrugged. "I don't know. No one does. I don't think any of them were very successful, and so now he relates to Joel's work. And supports him."

"Yes, so why aren't you supporting him? Joel happens to be one of your friends—most of the time," her mother reminded her.

"I suppose," Barri grumbled, still stinging from Joel's rejection. "I tried to talk to him after school, and he just took off."

"Maybe you should try again."

"No way." She saw her father's BMW pull into the driveway only to screech to a stop before reaching the garage. "What's going on?" Barri mumbled just as she noticed her brother's new

BMX bike flung carelessly on the concrete in front of the garage doors. "Uh-oh."

"Not again," Mrs. Gillette whispered.

"I'll get it!" Barri flew down the steps and sprinted across the dry grass and hot concrete in her bare feet. She grabbed the handlebars and pulled the chrome-and-red bicycle to safety while the BMW idled and her father steamed. Once the bike was out of the way, he drove into the garage.

Jeff, as if having a sixth sense, galloped down the path that cut through the laurel hedge of the backyard. He slid at the corner of the garage, nearly careening into Barri. Bonecrusher, the family's white-and-brown terrier, was fast on Jeff's heels, yapping excitedly.

"Uh-oh," Jeff murmured, his eyes rounding.

Bonecrusher, thrilled with the excitement charging the air, wagged his tail furiously and jumped on Barri.

"Down!" she yelled, then turned her attention to Jeff. "Are you crazy?" she whispered. "You know what Dad thinks about bikes in the driveway."

Her father cut the BMW's engine.

"I meant to put it away. Really. But the guys were playing ball in the park, and I just forgot."

"Boy, are you lucky," Jack Gillette said as he climbed out of the car. His eyes were focused on his son, and his expression didn't hold the hint of a smile. At nearly six feet, dressed in a three-piece business suit, his dark hair shot with gray, Barri's father cut an imposing figure.

Unfortunately he didn't scare Jeff. "Look, I'm

sorry," Jeff said, his lower lip protruding a fraction. "It won't happen again."

"You're sure?"

"Yeah! I said so, didn't I?"

Barri cringed. Her father's eyes narrowed thoughtfully. "Okay, Jeff, you're off the hook this time. There wasn't any damage. But if I find the bike out here again, you won't ride it for a week, and if someone runs over it, you pay to fix the bike *and* the car."

Jeff, to his credit, blanched a little at that, but nodded stiffly. "Okay."

Barri glanced at her mother, who had watched the entire scene from the porch.

Celia Gillette's dark brows rose. "I think your father needs a good five-mile run," she teased. "It sounds like he had a rough day."

"I just want Jeff to learn some responsibility!" Jack replied as he stepped onto the porch.

"Um-hm," Celia said with a knowing grin. "Come on, Jack. Barri will watch dinner, and Jeff will set the table. You and I can run off all our frustrations!" She slipped her arms around him and gave him a kiss. "What do ya say?" Her brown eyes twinkled. "Bet I can beat you to the bridge in the park."

"In your dreams."

Celia Gillette laughed. "Try me."

"You're on!" Together, still bantering back and forth, they walked into the house.

"You really lucked out!" Barri said, turning on her brother. "Dad wanted to murder you!"

"He did not!" Jeff argued.

"Yeah, well, if I were you, I wouldn't pull a stunt like that again if I wanted to live to see nine."

"Very funny." Jeff yanked the bike from Barri's hands and walked it into the garage. Barri didn't bother to pick up the fight again. It had already been a rotten day; there wasn't any need to make it worse.

Barri concentrated on her breathing, slowing her heart rate, calming herself as she and Melanie sat, cross-legged on Barri's bed. "Ready?" Barri finally asked, opening one eye.

"I guess."

"You go first."

"All right." Melanie stood, collecting herself for a second. A faraway look crossed her features. One hand clasped over her heart, Melanie strode across the carpet of Barri's bedroom and looked longingly out the window to the lawn below.

Felicia, who had been washing her face on the sill, stopped, one yellow-striped paw poised in mid-air, and cast Melanie a disdainful glance. Melanie didn't notice, not even when the cat plopped onto the floor and trotted indignantly out of the room. Melanie sighed dramatically and began: " 'O Romeo, Romeo, wherefore art thou Romeo? Deny thy father and refuse thy name. Or if thou wilt not, be but sworn my love and I'll no longer be a . . . a Montague.' "

" 'Capulet,' " Barri cut in.

"Wh-what?" Melanie blinked, as if waking up.

"Juliet's a Capulet. Romeo's a Montague."

"I know that." Melanie snapped, cross with herself. "Oh, what's wrong with me?" She yanked off her glasses and flung them on the wrinkled comforter of Barri's bed. "I can't concentrate! It's—it's these stupid glasses, and the audition, *and* Ward McKenna!" Melanie flopped onto Barri's bed and stared myopically at the ceiling. "I know I'm going to freeze the minute he walks onto the stage."

"You don't even know if we have to audition with him," Barri said, but her own heart was pounding miles a minute at the thought of actually being close to Ward.

"Oh, yes, I do. Geraldine's got the scoop."

"How does she know?"

Melanie pinned Barri with a knowing glare. One of her elegant blond brows arched. "Geraldine makes it her business to know. She's already in tight with the stage manager down at the theater, and she reads every scrap of publicity ever printed. Believe me, she knows!"

"And she told you the auditions are definitely with Ward?"

"She told Robert," Melanie said. "I overheard."

"So, you're not going out for *Thin Ice*? You haven't changed your mind?"

Melanie shook her head. "Nope. If you want the part of Jamie, my guess is, it's yours." Glancing at her watch, Melanie gasped. "I've got to go." She scooped up her books in a hurry. "See ya tomorrow!"

"D day," Barri moaned.

"It's not that bad."

"No, it's worse!" Barri watched Melanie fly down the stairs, then lay flat out on her bed, miserable at the thought of tryouts. She studied the cracks in her ceiling and decided that she'd try out for the part of Jamie the following day and then, next week, audition for Juliet.

"And so what happens if you land both parts?" she asked herself, flinging her arm over her eyes. Trouble, a voice in her mind replied. Big trouble!

CHAPTER FOUR

"NEXT! Gillette, Barbara!"

Barri gulped as she walked to center stage. Though she felt as if she had a million butterflies flitting around in her stomach, she tried not to show it.

In the front row of auditorium seats she could see Mr. Heifetz, Ms. Brookbank, and Joel. Mr. Heifetz was in his black turtleneck and slacks; Ms. Brookbank wore her favorite prim brown suit, white blouse, and large bowtie; and Joel, slouched down in his seat, was as irreverent as usual in his worn Levi's, shades, T-shirt and army jacket. All three pairs of eyes seemed glued to her.

Don't panic. This is all just part of being an actress, she told herself as she concentrated on her breathing.

"The same scene; act two, page fifty-five," Mr. Heifetz called out.

Barri flipped through the pages of her script, though she nearly had the scene memorized. She had already watched four girls, none of whom had ever been in one of Fillmore's productions, read from Joel's play. Though she'd whispered words of encouragement to those trying out, Barri felt that each girl had given a poor showing. The first had been so nervous, she'd stuttered, the second had lost her place, the third had been a statue—she hadn't moved a muscle and acted as if she'd actually taken root on the stage—and the fourth mumbled so horridly, no one past the second row had heard a word she'd said.

Now, it was Barri's turn. She glanced down at the page and visualized herself as Jamie, a young, sophisticated woman who'd thought she'd seen a ghost.

"I'm not kidding, Pete! And I'm not crazy, either. There's a spirit in this house, and I've seen it."

"Then you need to have those big brown eyes examined, Jamie," Robert, who was reading the part of Pete, Jamie's brother, responded.

"You don't believe me!" Barri gasped, her face pinched in rage, just as she imagined the character of Jamie would react. She fell into the role easily, and then during the rest of her audition, she wasn't aware of Joel or Mr. Heifetz or Ms. Brookbank. When she read the last line from the scene, she heard Joel's hoot of approval.

"Shh!" Ms. Brookbank scolded, sending him a dark look before saying, "Thank you, Barbara!"

Barri exited stage right and heard the other would-be actors whispering excitedly about her. "You were sensational!" Geraldine said when Barri plopped down beside her in the upper balcony.

"I hope so."

"A shoo-in," Melanie chimed in, though there was less enthusiasm in her voice.

"Something wrong?" Barri asked.

"Just Joel. He hasn't spoken to me in days!"

"Do you blame him? You practically begged for the part of Jamie," Barri reminded her.

"I know, I know." Melanie's face drew into a pout. "Come on, let's get out of here!"

"I can't leave yet," Geraldine whispered, just as yet another Jamie entered stage left. "Brookbank wants to talk to me about costumes." Rolling her eyes, Geraldine slumped back in her chair.

"Meet us at Prime-Time," Barri said, mentioning their favorite pizza parlor. Still elated about her audition, Barri wasn't about to let Geraldine's glum mood infect her. "We'll order a giant pepperoni, mushroom, and olive."

"I *hate* olives," Geraldine grumbled. "And I'm a vegetarian."

"Since when?" Barri asked.

"Since I read this!" Geraldine scrounged in her huge purse, found several beat-up magazines, and searched through them. Finally she found a copy of *Cool Vibes*, and flipped to a "New Age" article that stressed the avoidance of meat as a means to higher consciousness.

"That's crazy," Barri said as Melanie snatched the magazine and read.

"How do you know?"

"I don't, but—"

Geraldine stuffed the magazine back in her purse and shrugged. "It's your bodies—and spirits!"

"Okay, okay, how about extra cheese and mush-room?"

"You're on!" Geraldine said, just as auditions for the part of Pete began. Ms. Brookbank, who had volunteered to read Jamie's part, climbed the stairs and positioned herself center stage. "See ya later," Barri called over her shoulder as she and Melanie dashed up the aisle.

Prime-Time Pizza was located next door to Merion's local theater, The Playhouse. Decorated with black-and-white photos from scenes of the local productions, the pizza parlor was one of Barri's favorite places to hang out.

She and Melanie were seated opposite each other in a large booth with scarlet cushions and a slick, black table covered with a checkered cloth.

"Here you go," a waiter said as he scooped up the plastic playbill with their number on it and slid a steaming pizza onto the table.

"It looks great!" Barri said.

'It looks healthy," Melanie grumbled, wrinkling her nose.

"You might like it."

"I wouldn't bet on it," she said with a sigh as she selected a wedge.

Breathless, Geraldine hurried over to their table and slid into the booth next to Barri. "Watch out," she warned, grabbing a slice of the vegetarian con-coction. Strings of mozzarella cheese stretched from the huge center platter to her plate.

"Watch out for what?" Barri asked.

"Joel's on the warpath. Uh-oh!" Her eyes were

riveted to the door, which was flung open so hard, it banged against the wall. Joel, lips compressed, strode in. He spied the girls and stalked over to their table.

"So, where were you?" he asked, flipping his sunglasses onto his head and pinning Melanie with angry gray eyes.

"When?"

"You know when—during tryouts."

Melanie tilted her perfect chin up mutinously. "I was there."

"Not on the stage."

"I don't see what you're so hot about," Melanie snapped. "Barri did a terrific job. You should be thanking her instead of badgering me!"

Joel's gaze swung to Barri, and for a minute his temper seemed to fade. "Mel's right," he said. "You did a great job. Thanks."

Barri wanted to sink right through the floor. Joel hadn't said it, but obviously he thought she'd won the part of Jamie and would try her best in *Thin Ice*. And she would. *If* she didn't land the part of Juliet.

He dropped onto the bench next to Geraldine and leaned his head back against the cushion. "It just would've been nice if the rest of you guys could have shown some enthusiasm for the play—"

"It's got nothing to do with *Thin Ice*," Geraldine cut in.

"Yeah, yeah, I know. Don't start in with all that bull about *Romeo and Juliet*. I've heard enough about it to last me a lifetime."

"Oh, sure. And what if you weren't involved in

something right now?" Melanie asked. "If you weren't up to your eyeballs with *Thin Ice*, you would've been the first person down at The Playhouse."

Joel's jaw worked. "Well, it wouldn't have been because of some television star!"

Melanie opened her mouth to argue, then clamped it shut. "Think what you want."

"Hey—cut it out," Barri said, smiling despite the tension crackling at the table. Robert sauntered into the pizza parlor, spied the group, grabbed a nearby chair, twirled it around, and placed it deftly at the table where the girls were sitting. Straddling the chair backward, he scanned the table and motioned to a waitress. "We'll have another pitcher—diet cola. Right?" he asked, and Barri nodded. With a wry grin, Robert glanced at Joel and added, "Make sure it's a double."

"Very funny." Joel snickered.

Barri shoved the pizza toward Joel. "Have a slice," she offered, hoping to change the subject and dissipate some of the hostility radiating from him.

Joel glared at the pizza. "What *is* it?"

"Vegetarian delight."

"Are you kidding?" Joel groaned. "What happened to Canadian bacon, sausage, pepperoni, and ground beef?"

Geraldine skewered him with a pained look. "If you knew anything about health and psychic energy, Joel Amberson, you'd realize that—"

"Enough already!" Joel held his palms up. "It's fine—great." He grabbed a large slice "In fact, it's just what I would've ordered." He took a huge bite and, wincing theatrically, swallowed with obvious and overly dramatic difficulty.

Barri giggled. Melanie laughed outright, and even Geraldine, still trying to look peeved, chuckled. Robert shook his head.

"So tell us," Barri suggested, "in reasonable terms, mind you, how the rest of auditions went."

"About as bad as can be expected," Joel replied.

"No." Barri wouldn't believe it.

"Wanna bet? Heifetz is even thinking about casting Ms. Brookbank as Jamie's twelve-year-old sister, Liz."

Barri rolled her eyes to the ceiling and tried not to laugh. The thought of Ms. Brookbank in her subdued wool suits, neatly coiled brown hair, sensible shoes, and carefully applied makeup, playing the part of an energetic tomboy was absurd.

Even Geraldine cracked up. "Be serious."

"I am," Joel mocked, just as Rich and two other boys who played on the soccer team joined the group. Rich's dusty-blond hair was still damp from his shower, his face flushed from the workout.

"Hi!" Barri called, trading places with Geraldine so that she could sit next to Rich.

He plopped down and slung his arm familiarly around her shoulder. "How'd it go?" he asked.

"Great. And practice?"

"It was tough. Coach Morris was a bear."

"A Kodiak," his friend amended.

Rich reached for a piece of pizza, but as his gaze dropped to the platter, his hand stopped midair.

"Don't ask," Barri advised quickly, "unless you want a detailed speech on 'New Age' karma."

Rich winked at Barri, and she felt positively warm inside. "So," he asked, ignoring the pizza completely, "did you get the part?"

"I don't know yet."

"It's in the bag," Robert predicted.

"Only Joel knows for sure," Melanie said, casting Joel an interested glance.

"And he's not talking," Joel said with a crooked grin. "Results of the audition will be posted next Monday at the usual place."

"Since when do you play by the rules?" Robert wanted to know.

"A person could die before Monday," Geraldine pointed out.

"Let's hope not." Joel snapped his glasses back onto his nose. "Unfortunately *Thin Ice* needs every warm body it can get!"

CHAPTER FIVE

"YOU got it!" Melanie cried. Jumping up and down excitedly, her blond hair flying, she read the cast list posted next to the auditorium doors. "You're Jamie!" She hugged Barri. "Congratulations!"

"Thanks!" For a few brief seconds, Barri's spirits soared. Until she realized that suddenly her life had become very complicated. How could she possibly try out for Juliet now that she really was Jamie Winston?

"I knew you'd get it," Melanie said, calming a little. No longer wearing glasses, her cheeks flushed, she was pleased for Barri. "No one else was even in the running!"

"So, who else is in the cast?" Barri asked, almost afraid to look.

"Let's see—Kim Landis, Matthew Taylor, Brigg Nelson, Annie Lorenzini . . ."

Barri sighed while Melanie rattled off the names of kids she had never heard of before. Not one Thespian, but then, she'd known that much on the day of tryouts. Kurt, Melanie, Geraldine, and Robert hadn't bothered auditioning. "They all must be

freshmen," Melanie said, eyeing the list one last
time. She offered Barri an encouraging grin. "You'll
be great!"

"Unless I have to bow out," Barri worried aloud.

"Bow out? Why?"

Chewing nervously on her lower lip, Barri
glanced over her shoulder to make sure no one
was within earshot. "I haven't really decided not
to audition for Juliet."

"*What!* You're joking, right?"

"No—"

"But what if you get the part?" Melanie asked,
clearly alarmed by Barri's news.

"Then I guess I'll have to tell Joel and Mr. Heifetz and Ms. Brookbank."

"Oh, wow," Melanie whispered, her face suddenly draining of color. "Joel will tar and feather
you."

"And Mr. Heifetz?"

Melanie made a face. "Simple. He probably could
kick you out of the Thespians or flunk you out of
drama class, but that would be too easy. No," she
decided, "since this is one of Joel's plays you're
walking out on, my guess is he'll make sure you
never land another part in a Fillmore production
again." Barri groaned. Though she knew Melanie
was just kidding, she felt absolutely awful. She'd
already turned in her audition slip at the Playhouse
Theatre, but if she really wanted to, she could still
back out and give up on the chance of a lifetime.

Even though she hadn't yet decided to try out
for Juliet, she'd already started gearing up—even
the outfit she was wearing wasn't her usual style,

with its full sleeves and soft pastel colors. She'd put on the ruffled dress that morning because it seemed romantic and soft, reminding her of Juliet's pure, tragic love. But now that she'd landed the part of Jamie, not only was she dressed all wrong, but she had some serious thinking to do.

"Look at it this way," Melanie said, sobering. "I really should get the part of Juliet."

"Why?"

"Because I've always played the tragic heroines around here, Barri. You know that! You've done lighter stuff—comedy. . . . "

"I know but—"

Melanie affected a long-suffering look and started quoting from *Romeo and Juliet*: " 'I have a faint cold fear thrills through my veins that almost freezes up the heat of life.' "

"I get the picture," Barri murmured.

The morning bell clanged, and Melanie tossed off her tragic persona as she headed toward her locker. "Cheer up," she called brightly. "It could be worse."

"Don't tell me—it could be raining!" Barri glanced through the tall windows by the staircase and noticed a few gray clouds attempting to block out the autumn sun.

"No, silly. I mean *really* worse. You might not have gotten the part of Jamie or the part of Juliet."

That, Barri thought glumly as she wended her way through the crowded halls toward the chemistry lab, would be better than facing Joel Amberson if I have to tell him I can't portray his protagonist in his best play to date.

* * *

"I don't see what the big deal is," Rich said later as he drove Barri home in his 1953 Dodge pickup. The truck was a relic, but Rich spent all his free time fixing it up. When he wasn't playing ball or going to school, he was banging out the fenders and polishing the chrome. Freshly painted a metallic candy-apple red, the truck's hood glinted in the afternoon sun. He shifted down and continued, "So, you get both parts. It's kind of like sports."

"What?" For a minute she thought he was kidding. But the look on his face as he squinted against the afternoon sunshine streaming through the windshield was dead serious. "No way."

"Sure. Suppose you're good at football *and* soccer. And suppose you make both teams. Then you've got to make a choice, right? And if you choose soccer, the guys on the football team are mad, not to mention the coach. Same with football—if you decide to be a running back instead of a soccer forward, the guys on the soccer team are steamed."

"It's more complicated than that," Barri argued, but knew he'd made a valid point.

"Maybe. But if you ask me—" his gaze slid to hers for a second—"your real problem is Joel."

"He's only part of it."

"The major part of it. He's your friend, and you don't want to let him down. You think everyone else has abandoned him."

"They have."

"Well, at least they were honest about it."

"Meaning?"

"You're the only one who tried out while planning to ditch him."

"I won't ditch him!"

"Not even if you get the part in—whatever it is?"

She glared at him through narrowed eyes. "You know what it is."

A crooked smile crossed Rich's grin. "Yeah, I know, I was just giving you a hard time." He flipped on the radio, and the latest hit from Bon Jovi filled the interior of his pickup.

"I don't need a hard time, thank you very much."

"Hey—I'm sorry. Okay? It's just that I think you're getting all worked up over nothing."

Barri, who couldn't stay glum for long, grudgingly agreed. "You're right, I guess."

"As always."

"Give me a break," Barri said, but she giggled.

"So—do you really want some advice?"

"I suppose."

"I think you'd better be straight with Joel."

"Straight with him?"

"Yeah. Call him and tell him what you're doing."

"He'll go through the roof."

"No doubt," Rich thought aloud, cranking on the steering wheel and guiding the car into the curved driveway of the Gillette home. "Hey, what's going on?"

Barri followed his gaze to the second story. Where once there had been a sliding glass door to her parents' bedroom, there was now a huge gaping hole covered with plastic.

Barri sighed. "Mom's refurbishing the house, trying to make it look just like it did in the eighteen hundreds. But she's run into a couple of problems because she wants the house modern, too. You know, with running water, electricity, and gas."

"And cable TV?"

"Right," Barri said with a grin. "The essentials."

"So, what's with the window?"

"I'm not sure, but she mentioned something about putting in French doors. However, there's some problem with the size of the doors and the original windows." She picked up her book bag and cocked her head toward the house. "Want to come inside for a few minutes?"

"I can't," he said with a sigh. "I'd like to, but I'm late already. There's a big family dinner tonight— my grandma's birthday."

Barri tried to hide her disappointment with a nod. "Okay, see you tomorrow."

"Sure." He offered her a grin and wrapped his arms around her so quickly, she gasped, then laughed. When he kissed her, she tingled a little but wondered why skyrockets didn't explode in her head. "I'll call you later," he promised when he finally let her go.

Barri slid out of the car and waved as he drove off. He *was* special, and cute, and a basketball and soccer star. So why wasn't she absolutely sure she loved him?

"Two little lovebirds sitting in a tree. *K-I-S-S-I-N-G!*" Jeff sang, off key, from one of the upper limbs of an apple tree in the side yard.

Barri froze. "What're you doing up there?" she demanded, dropping her books on the driveway. "Spying?"

Jeff just laughed, and she wanted to scream! "I don't know why someone in this house hasn't stuffed you down the laundry chute—or worse!"

"Wanna try?"

"Sure."

Jeff hooted. "You'd never catch me."

That did it! Despite her ruffled "Juliet" dress, she grabbed hold of the lowest branch and started climbing for all she was worth. Her new shoes slid on the gnarly bark, but she made some headway, and Jeff, a look of sheer horror on his face, started scrambling upward to the smaller, less sturdy branches. "When I get hold of you—" she threatened, although she was already seeing the humor in the situation.

Glaring down at her, the dangling shoelace of his Nikes right in front of her nose, Jeff demanded, "What?"

She grinned from ear to ear. "I'll haul you out of this tree and down the block to Michelle Anderson's house and tell her you have a crush on her!"

"No way!"

She grabbed hold of his ankle, and he shrieked. "Then give it a rest about the *K-I-S-S-I-N-G* stuff, okay?"

"Okay," he grumbled. "Besides, I *hate* Michelle Anderson!"

"Sure you do," Barri said, smirking.

"She's a four-eyes!"

"Maybe she'd like to hear you say it."

"She already knows! You're just mad 'cause I saw you with Rich!"

"That's right," Barri said sweetly.

"Barbara! Jeff! What in heaven's name are you doing up there?" Mrs. Gillette jogged up the driveway and snatched a towel from the backseat of her car. Sweat dotted her forehead as she looped the fluffy white towel around her neck. As usual, she was wearing a coordinated jogging suit, this time in a pale yellow shade that complimented her dark hair and tanned skin.

Barri hopped to the ground. "What's it called when the Russian and American leaders sit down and talk things out—*detente*? Well, Jeff and I were having a little brother-sister *detente* of our own."

"We were not." Jeff argued, jumping from the lowest branch and landing with a thud in the middle of the yard. "Barri was going to stuff me down the laundry chute."

Mrs. Gillette sighed and dabbed at her forehead with the edge of her towel. "I think I've heard enough."

Barri ignored Jeff's comment and raced up to the front porch. A wide grin stretched across her lips. "Guess what?" she asked her mother.

"I give. What?"

"You're looking at Jamie Winston."

"Jamie *who*?" Jeff demanded.

Mrs. Gillette's brows pulled together before a smile tugged at the corners of her mouth. "You got the part!" Thrilled, she hugged Barri.

"So what?" Jeff grumbled.

"It's the lead," her mother pointed out. "I think this calls for a celebration dinner!"

"Pizza!" Jeff cried.

Barri's mother laughed. "I was thinking more

about steak Diane or veal *cordon bleu* or scampi
in garlic—"

Jeff rolled his eyes. "Some celebration."

Mrs. Gillette glanced up at the second story. "See
that?" she asked, pointing toward the hole. "Believe it or not, we're going to celebrate the fact
that I actually found a pair of French doors that
will fit. They'll be delivered tomorrow."

"Good," Jeff said, his brow furrowing into a deep
scowl as he eyed the plastic sheeting. "Is that thing
burglar-proof?"

"I hope so," Barri's mother said with a laugh.

"Maybe Bonecrusher should sleep in your room
tonight," Jeff offered.

"Oh, that's great," Barri chortled. "Bonecrusher
the watchdog!" Still giggling, she asked, "Is it okay
if Melanie has dinner with us? We have some rehearsing to do."

"Sure. Did she get a part, too?"

Barri could have swallowed her tongue. "No—
uh—we're reading from *Romeo and Juliet.*

Mrs. Gillette's eyes darkened, and she stared at
Barri as if she didn't think she'd heard her cor-
rectly. "You're *still* going out for that? What about
this part of Jamie? Won't it conflict?"

"Not unless I get lucky."

"Barbara—" her mother said in a serious, moth-
erly tone.

"Really, Mom. Don't worry about it! I can handle
everything," Barri said, sounding much more confident than she felt. Scooping her books from the
driveway, she headed for the front door. "Did I get
any mail today?" she called over her shoulder.

"Just a couple of magazines, I think."

Jeff's eyes twinkled. "What're you waiting for—a love letter?"

"Oh, save me," Barri groaned as she started into the house.

"Wait a minute. I forgot," her mother called after her. "Joel called about a half hour ago. He wants you to call him back. He wouldn't say what it was about."

"Probably the play," Barri guessed.

"You'd think he would have told me the news," Mrs. Gillette thought aloud, then added, "I suppose he didn't want to ruin things by telling me first."

"Right," Barri said, her spirits sinking again. She wasn't up to talking to Joel, not when she hadn't decided how to break the news that she still planned to audition for Juliet.

In the kitchen Barri riffled through the mail, disappointed that she didn't have an answer on the soap opera contest. Though the deadline for turning in the entries had only been last week, she'd hoped to hear something. "It'll probably be months," she told herself glumly.

She snatched a pear, apple muffin, and a diet soda from the refrigerator, then dashed upstairs and opened her geometry book. She had to get through her homework before dinner so she could practice with Melanie. Fleetingly she considered phoning Joel, but decided to wait until later. Instead, she sat cross-legged on the floor, placed her hands on her knees, exhaled, and closed her eyes. Yoga always helped her concentrate on her lines and aided her in finding the true inner self of her character.

As she took in another deep breath, Barri forgot about her homework and Joel.

CHAPTER SIX

"ISN'T he cute?" Melanie sighed, reaching for a handful of popcorn as the credits for "Three for Breakfast" rolled over the image of Ward McKenna and one of his costars. Ward, laughing, his blue eyes dancing mischievously, was in the act of tossing a water balloon at Cissie, his love interest in the show.

"The cutest," Barri admitted without taking her eyes off the screen.

"And next week, *next week*, we get to meet him!" Melanie grabbed a throw pillow off the couch, held it tightly against her chest, closed her eyes, and with a blissful sigh flopped onto her back. "I can't believe that he'd give up the show for a play in Merion!"

"He's not giving it up. Where did I read about him?" Barri wondered aloud as she riffled through the newspapers, scripts, and baseball cards strewn across the coffee table in the family room of the Gillette home. The house was still filled with the scent of roast poultry, and clanging noises from the kitchen indicated that Barri's mother hadn't quite cleaned up the supper dishes. "Oh, here it is." She retrieved the latest edition of *Teen Idols* from the stack. "It says that the producers of 'Three for Breakfast' were worried about an actor's strike, so they taped a lot of shows over the summer. Here—" She shoved the article, accompanied by a studio shot of Ward, under Melanie's nose.

"Oh, wow," Melanie said, studying the picture. "Isn't he to die for?"

Barri grinned. "Well, actually, he is. I'm thinking of trying out for the play with Juliet's death scene."

Melanie shuddered. "The death scene—why?"

"Think about it. Ward's going to be at the audition, playing the part of Romeo, right?"

"Right." Melanie was still confused. She munched another mouthful of popcorn.

"Remember the line—how's it go? 'I will kiss thy lips. Haply some poison yet doth hang on them to make me die with a restorative.' " Barri giggled. "And I'll get to kiss Ward McKenna!"

"Barri, that's downright underhanded!" Melanie gasped, her blue eyes crinkling at the corners.

"Oh, you're just mad 'cause you didn't think of it first."

Melanie sighed. "Maybe, but he'll just be lying there, pretending to be dead."

Barri lifted a shoulder. "Who cares?"

Melanie struck a dramatic pose. "I do, because I'd do anything, *anything*, to be his Juliet." She let out a tragic sigh, and her face filled with suffering. "I just have to get the part!"

"Hey, are you guys done yet?" Jeff asked, sauntering into the family room from the kitchen.

"We were going to run through our lines."

"Well, I want to watch the game." He dropped onto the couch, picked up the remote control, and punched a button, changing the station on the television. The voice of a major league baseball announcer filled the room as a player stepped up to bat on the screen.

"Okay, okay, we can work in the kitchen," Barri decided. Jeff's nose had been out of joint ever since dinner, when the conversation had revolved around Barri, Melanie, and the two upcoming plays.

Melanie picked up her copy of *The Complete Works of William Shakespeare*, and the girls headed to the kitchen, where Mrs. Gillette was still filling the dishwasher. The table had been cleared, but now, instead of dishes, it was covered with swatches of cloth and wallpaper books.

"Let me guess," Barri's mother quipped. "You girls came in to help."

Barri rolled her eyes. "If you want us to."

Celia shook her head. "Not tonight. We're celebrating, remember? But tomorrow you're back on duty."

"Thanks, Mom."

Mrs. Gillette spied Melanie's book. "If you want to rehearse, why don't you go outside to the patio—you can take out some hot chocolate or tea."

"Cocoa!" Melanie said quickly.

Barri heated water in the microwave oven, then

added the mix. She and Melanie each grabbed a steaming mug and backtracked through the family room.

Outside, the sky was streaked with lavender. A slight breeze rustled through the dry leaves of the maple and oak trees. Bonecrusher was lying in his favorite spot in a hole he'd excavated beneath a juniper bush. He stretched and yawned as Melanie settled into a padded lawn chair. Barri gazed at the dusky twilight and imagined how Juliet would feel, alone on a balcony, staring at the coming night, waiting for Romeo. Goose bumps rose on Barri's arms, and she imagined the sound of hoof-beats, of rustling underbrush, of Romeo's calling to her. . . ."

"Barri? Can we get into this?" Melanie asked, breaking into her thoughts.

"Wha—oh, yeah. Sure," Barri said quickly, feeling as if she *were* Juliet. She sat in one of the chairs surrounding a glass-topped umbrella table. Bonecrusher immediately started whining at the door. "You want to go inside?" she asked the scrappy little dog. "I think it's safe now."

"Why'd your mom kick him out?"

"Because of the Cornish game hens. Any time that dog is near poultry, he whines and begs and makes a general nuisance of himself." Barri opened the glass door, and Bonecrusher, nails clicking on the hardwood, charged inside, making a beeline for the kitchen.

"Okay, let's get started," Melanie suggested, flipping through the pages. "You go first—here's the death scene." She scanned the lines and wrinkled her aristocratic nose. "You know, it's not really very long."

Barri peered over her shoulder. "You're right," she agreed, knowing she'd need a longer monologue in order to convince the director to cast her. "I'd better do something else."

Nodding thoughtfully, Melanie said, "I hate to keep saying this, but I really feel this part was made for me. All the pain and suffering, the anguish. It's, it's just so—"

"So Melanie Todd?"

"Right."

"Come on, get serious," Barri said, but she knew Melanie was right. Even though Melanie hadn't suffered much in her life, she really knew how to empathize with tragic characters—how to "feel" their torture.

Melanie cleared her throat. "Okay, I'm sorry, I got off track." She glanced over the death scene again. "You know, this is really a great scene—even if you're not going to use it. Let's start with it—just to get into the mood."

"Okay." Taking the book from Melanie's hands, Barri studied the lines, closed her eyes for a second, again embracing the character of Juliet, feeling the night surround her with the blackness of Romeo's death. " 'Go, get thee hence, for I will not away.' " She glanced to the brick patio, where she imagined Romeo lay. Gasping, she whispered, " 'What's here? A cup clos'd in my true love's hand? Poison, I see, hath been his timeless end.' "

"Bravo!" Joel's voice cut through the encroaching darkness.

Barri nearly jumped out of her skin. Her voice died, and her concentration disintegrated. Not now, she thought, color rising in her cheeks.

"Uh-oh," Melanie whispered, casting Barri a worried glance.

Joel, standing in the open door, a thick script tucked under his arm, was staring hard at Barri. "What's going on here?" he asked.

"We're rehearsing," Barri replied, feeling about two inches tall.

"Without a script?" He tossed a copy of *Thin Ice* onto the umbrella table.

Barri swallowed hard.

Melanie glanced nervously at her friend. "I think that was my cue to exit—stage left."

"You don't have to leave," Joel protested.

"I know," Melanie said, bristling as she shoved her book into her bag and slung the strap over her shoulder. "And as long as we're telling people what they can or can't do, *you* can stop acting like a pompous jerk. Barri has the right to do anything she wants." With a toss of her golden hair she said, "I'll see you guys tomorrow at school." She slipped through the house, and Barri heard her saying thank-you and good-night to her mother and Jeff.

"So—what's up?" Joel asked.

Knowing the ax was about to fall, Barri braced herself. The look on Joel's face was positively thunderous. "I called you this afternoon," he said.

"I know." Biting her lower lip, Barri said, "I was going to call you back after Melanie went home."

"Sure."

"Really."

With a tired sigh he sat on a corner of the chaise lounge and plowed his fingers through his hair. "Why, Barri?" he asked, obviously hurt, his eyes searching her face. "Why are you going out for Juliet when you're already Jamie?"

Barri wanted to die. She studied her hands nervously and forced her fingers not to fidget. "Because it's too good a part to turn down."

"And Jamie?"

"I really want to play Jamie—really!" She looked up at Joel and grinned. "She's your best character ever."

"Why do I expect to hear *but*?"

Barri rolled her eyes. "But I can't give up the chance to play Juliet opposite—"

"I know. Ward McKenna. I tell you, if I hear that guy's name one more time, I'm gonna throw up!" One of Joel's legs was bouncing rapidly up and down, and his jaw was set, his mouth pinched. "So what's going to happen if you get the part—huh? What then? You can't play both!"

"You don't know that!" Barri said quickly. "I was at a theater festival last summer, and I saw three plays, all of which were played by the same troupe. An actor would play a part in the afternoon when the modern plays were performed; then later that night, he'd do something classical."

"Did the same actors play the leads?"

"No, but—"

"And were the plays running opposite each other?"

"No, but *Thin Ice* will be over before *Romeo and Juliet* gets started!"

"But the rehearsals will conflict. The first read-through is Monday." A muscle worked in his jaw, and Barri realized Joel was having trouble hanging onto his temper. Patience had never been his long suit.

To avoid staring at him, she glanced around and noticed for the first time that the sky had turned dark. Stars winked, and a slice of crescent moon hung high in the sky. The wind, cooler now, cut through her sweatshirt and ruffled Joel's black hair.

"You know," he said, "you've put me in a bad spot."

"Why?"

"I should tell Mr. Heifetz what you're doing."

"And then?"

"And then he'll recast the part of Jamie." Joel stood, his hands shoved deep into the pockets of his faded jeans. "But that will ruin the play. You saw the other actresses who tried out. They were horrible."

"Not so bad—"

"Horrible! You and I both know it. A couple of the freshmen might develop, but they're too young and green for Jamie!" He glanced over his shoulder. "You know, at least Melanie was honest. I could've kicked her for not trying out, but this is worse." Shaking his head, he reached for the door.

"Joel!" Barri cried, chasing after him.

"What?"

"I didn't mean to hurt you, and I didn't mean to foul up the play. I just want to do what's best for my career."

"I know," Joel said tersely. "So do I. See ya." Without another word he stalked through the house and out the front door. Barri followed him but stopped in the front yard, watching as he jogged down the darkened street.

He disappeared around the corner, and Barri felt tears sting the backs of her eyes. Joel was one of her best friends, but he just didn't understand—or did he?

Feeling absolutely dejected, she walked around the side of the house to the patio, cleared off the half-full cups of hot chocolate and Joel's script.

"Trouble?" Her mother asked, when Barri rinsed the dirty mugs and stacked them in the dishwasher. Mrs. Gillette was seated at the kitchen table, taking notes as she sorted through a stack of wallpaper books, swatches, and paint samples.

"A little."

"What're you going to do?"

Barri shook her head. Her dark brown curls swept her cheek. "I don't know," she admitted with a heartfelt sigh. "I just don't know."

"You could call Kelly or Aunt Laura," her mother suggested. "Maybe they can give you some advice.

Besides, I think they'd both like to hear about *Thin Ice*."

"Maybe I will," Barri said as she tucked the copy of the script under her arm and hurried upstairs. Felicia tagged after her. At the door of her room Barri stopped, tossed the script onto her bed, then headed straight to her parents' room. Decorated in hunter green and tan, with polished plank floors and a thick lamb's wool throw rug, the room was warm and homey—except, of course, for the plastic-draped hole leading to the veranda. Barri parked herself in an antique rocking chair and wrapped her mother's favorite patchwork quilt over her shoulders. Shivering slightly, she dialed her sister, at Connecticut College.

"Hello?"

Barri smiled at the sound of Kelly's voice. Though they'd often fought, they had been best friends and stuck up for each other more times than she could remember.

"Hi, Kell."

"Barri!" her sister cried. "I was just about to call you!"

"You were?"

"Um-hmm. I needed a break from the books. I've had it with amoeba and protozoa."

Barri giggled, some of her glum mood disappearing as she pictured Kelly, her brown hair pulled into a ponytail, in jeans and a sweatshirt, lying on the floor as she poured over stacks and stacks of biology books. "I thought you liked all that stuff."

"I do—but enough's enough. Besides, I thought it was time to check in at home. What's up?"

"Well, I got the lead in Joel's latest play, *Thin Ice*."

"That's great!"

"Yes and no," Barri admitted, launching into her tale about the two plays, Joel's black mood, and the chance to work with Ward McKenna.

"I knew Ward," Kelly said. "He was in the class ahead of me."

"Isn't he just the cutest!"

"I didn't think so at the time," Kelly admitted, "but he's, uh, grown up a little since high school."

"A lot!" Barri said.

"I don't blame you for wanting to work with him, but I can see why Joel's upset. You probably shouldn't even have tried out for *Thin Ice*."

"So now you tell me."

"Maybe you should have called me *before* the deed was done."

"Maybe," Barri agreed halfheartedly.

"I don't know that there's anything you can do."

"Thanks a lot." Barri sighed; then, because she didn't want to dwell on what was quickly becoming an insurmountable problem, she changed the subject, asked about college, and fifteen minutes later, when her mother walked into the bedroom, handed her the receiver. "It's your other daughter," she said, before tossing off the quilt and padding down the hall to her room.

Felicia, who had been hiding under the bed, trotted after her and hopped lithely onto the windowsill in Barri's room.

Barri petted the fat tabby, then turned to her closet. As she did whenever she was playing a part, Barri searched through her wardrobe, matching skirts, sweaters, shoes, and slacks, trying to find the right outfits that would make her look and feel the part of Jamie Winston—a young socialite who's seen her dead boyfriend's ghost.

Very few of Barri's clothes were quite up to the lofty standards of Jamie Winston, but Barri put together a few outfits that might work. "Be grateful you're not Juliet," she told herself as she matched a white silk blouse with a narrow black skirt. "You only have one dress that's flouncy and romantic. It would mean a whole new wardrobe."

Holding the outfit together, she twirled in front of the mirror, then looked at Felicia. "What do ya think?"

Felicia twitched her tail.

"Right, red earrings and shoes and belt! Silver would be better, but I don't have any silver shoes." Barri hung the skirt and blouse near the front of the closet. "That should get me through tomorrow." She closed her eyes, imagining herself as Jamie Winston. Without conscious thought she straightened her shoulders, lifted her chin, and curved her lips into a gentle smile that wasn't her usual wide grin. "Perfect!" she told herself as she saw her reflection. She *was* Jamie Winston. Unless she got lucky and *became* Juliet Capulet!

Picking up the copy of *Thin Ice*, she opened to the first page. There, in Joel's distinctive scrawl, hastily scratched diagonally across the page, was a simple message: "Barri—Thanks for having faith in me and *Thin Ice*. You're a real friend!"

"Joel—oh, no," Barri moaned, feeling glum again. She snapped the script shut and closed her eyes. "How," she wondered aloud, "did I get myself into this mess?"

CHAPTER SEVEN

THE rest of the week at school was awful! Joel barely spoke a word to anyone, including Barri. Geraldine was in a foul mood because of costume problems for *Thin Ice*, and Melanie could talk of nothing but Ward McKenna. Rumor had it that Ward was in town, and Melanie was determined to find out where he was staying.

To make matters worse, Rich hadn't been his usual happy-go-lucky self. The soccer team was scheduled to play Colton High School, Fillmore's arch rival, and Rich spent every free minute practicing with the team.

Barri was never so glad that a week was over! When the last bell rang on Friday afternoon, she slammed her locker shut, hiked her book bag over her shoulder, and dashed for the doors. She met Melanie in the parking lot.

"Let's go down to The Playhouse and see if maybe Ward's showed up," Melanie suggested.

"I can't."

"Why not?"

"The soccer game—remember? I thought we were going together."

Melanie rolled her eyes and yanked open the door of her Mustang. "I forgot. You know how I feel about sports."

"But I promised Rich. Come on, it'll be fun."

"Fun, she says."

"Please." Barri grinned and giggled. "Besides, I brought along a copy of the *Times*! There's a whole section of reviews of the latest Broadway shows."

"Okay, okay. Enough arm-twisting!" Melanie lifted her palms as if in surrender. "You win. But let's go home, change, and grab something to eat."

"You're on," Barri said, feeling better than she had since trying out for *Thin Ice*. "My treat."

"Good. I'm still broke." Melanie slid into the car and flicked on the ignition.

"I can't believe it."

"It's my dad. If you ask me, he's taking this austerity program too far."

"Why?"

"Oh, I don't know, something about the stock market."

"Yeah, my dad's been a little nervous, too," Barri agreed. "Ever since Black Monday."

"Right. Anyway, Dad cut my allowance in half, and I've got this great outfit down at The Fashion Connection on layaway." Melanie smiled dreamily. "It's the greatest. I want to wear it for the audition on Monday." She grinned at Barri. "I could pick it up today if you don't mind."

Barri laughed. "Mind? Are you kidding? Let's go!"

"Good!" Melanie stepped on the throttle. She cruised out of the parking lot and headed toward town.

Barri fiddled with the radio until she found a station playing the latest hit from the Pet Shop Boys. The song's quick tempo filled the car, and Barri rolled her window down, enjoying the warm September air that rushed against her cheeks and ruffled her hair. "T.G.I.F.," she said, sighing.

In town Melanie parked on the street near the boutique. As she and Barri walked past the window display, Barri stopped dead in her tracks. Against a backdrop curtain of pink silk was a mannequin dressed in a gorgeous, sophisticated black dress with a wide silver belt. A silver bag dangled from the mannequin's lifeless fingers, and matching pumps covered her feet. A white enamel bracelet painted with fine streaks of silver and gold completed the outfit.

"Perfect," Barri whispered, nose pressed to the glass.

"What?"

"All those accessories! They're just what Jamie Winston would wear!"

Melanie glanced dubiously at the mannequin. "If you say so. Come on." Tugging on Barri's arm, she pushed open the door, causing a small brass bell over the threshold to ring, announcing their entrance.

"Melanie!" A petite saleswoman with flaming red hair clapped her hands together when she saw the girls. "You're back for the jumpsuit!"

"Is it ready?"

The salesclerk nodded briskly. "All the alterations have been made. It's in the back."

Barri's eyes rounded. "They altered it for you *on layaway*?"

Melanie shrugged. "They know my mom."

That explained it. Melanie's mother, Cassandra Todd, was one of the most fashionable women in Merion. Cassandra hosted garden club luncheons, attended every charity ball in Merion, and spent a lot of evenings in New York at the ballet, symphony, and the theater.

"Here you go!" The saleslady unzipped a plastic bag for Melanie's inspection.

"What do you think?" Melanie asked Barri. She pulled out a shimmery copper-colored jumpsuit.

"It's gorgeous!"

"I decided I couldn't live without it—austerity program or no austerity program!" Melanie paid the balance of her layaway bill and started for the door, but Barri lingered at the display case.

"Is there something I can help you with?" the saleswoman asked eagerly.

On impulse Barri replied, "I just wondered if you had those shoes in size six."

"I'll check if you like."

"Please," Barri said, ignoring her conscience. The shoes and belt were a fortune. Unfortunately they fit perfectly, and the matching purse, earrings, and necklace looked great on her.

"You've got to have them." Melanie declared.

"Could—could you hold them for me?" Barri asked. "I've got to check with my mom."

The saleswoman's gaze swept from Barri to Melanie and back again. "Of course," she said. "Just call me. My name's Pam."

"I will," Barri promised, wondering if she'd gone out of her mind as she and Melanie walked the two blocks to The Fifties, where they each ordered a vanilla Coke and fries.

"I don't know what got into me," Barri said, dunking a french fry into a deep glob of catsup.

Melanie's blue eyes danced. "It's simple. You've been repressed too long."

Barri groaned, thinking of the combined cost of everything. "Maybe Mom will buy me the belt and shoes for my birthday. I'll be sixteen next month."

"That's right. Sure she will. Why not?" Melanie said as Elvis Presley's voice crooned "Blue Suede Shoes."

Why not? Barri thought. Because we're remodeling the house, because Kelly's going to college, because Dad and Mom are thinking about taking a vacation in Europe next year.

Barri swirled her straw in her Coke and glanced at the clock over the soda fountain. Her heart did a nosedive. Five-fifteen! "Oh, no!"

"What?" Melanie glanced around the crowded restaurant, wondering what had gotten into her friend.

"The game! It's at five-thirty! If I miss it, Rich'll kill me!"

"No, he won't!"

"But I missed the last one!" Feeling like an absolute louse, she dropped some bills onto the counter, grabbed Melanie's arm, and propelled her out of the restaurant. "Come on!"

Melanie drove Barri home in record time. Half an hour later, they were back at the school, half running down the grassy bank to the bleachers near the soccer field. The game was already well under way. Players for both teams—Colton in blue and gold, Fillmore in crimson and white—ran up and down the grassy field, kicking or heading the ball quickly toward their goals.

Barri slid onto a bench about three rows up, between parents and students, in the Fillmore section of the bleachers.

"Come on, Eagles!" a burly man behind her shouted.

"Let's go!" a spunky blond cheerleader cried.

Barri squinted to get a glimpse of Rich, and her heart swelled at the sight of him. Wearing the crimson uniform of the Fillmore Eagles, Rich positioned himself in front of the goal. His face flushed, his hair damp from sweat, he didn't take his eyes off the ball as it was kicked from one side of the field to the other.

"He *is* cute," Melanie admitted as she squeezed onto the bench beside Barri.

Barri smiled to herself. "He is, isn't he?"

Melanie slid her sunglasses onto her nose. "But then, he's no Ward McKenna."

"He doesn't need to be." Barri replied.

"Save me," Melanie muttered, her gaze barely on the game. Melanie wasn't into sports. Neither was Barri. Not really. But she tried—for Rich's sake. Melanie snatched Barri's copy of the *Times* from her backpack and thumbed through the entertainment section. Barri, though her eyes wandered to the reviews, tried to keep her attention on the game. The players drove the ball up and down the field, and Rich made several brilliant saves. The score jockeyed back and forth. By the second period the score was Colton five and Fillmore four. Down by one.

"I hope we don't lose," Barri whispered to Melanie.

Melanie lifted a shoulder. "It won't be the end of the world."

"It will be to Rich."

"That's Rich's problem," Melanie said, unconcerned. "You know what they say, 'You win some, you lose some.'"

Barri couldn't help but feel a little annoyed as she glanced at Melanie. Though sports weren't important to Melanie, they were to Rich. And as for losing, Barri had yet to see Melanie lose an audition without feeling blue.

"Come on, you Eagles! Get on the ball! Hey, goalie, watch what you're doing!" a man directly behind Barri yelled at the top of his lungs. Barri's gaze swung back to the field, where the opposing team, the Colton Cougars, were driving the ball toward the goal.

Rich was tense, his body ready, his eyes glued

to the ball as it was passed from one player to the next.

One Colton forward moved swiftly downfield, dodging a block by a Fillmore defender. Colton was in scoring position. Rich blocked the first shot, deflecting it with his knee, but the ball slammed back against the forward who passed it across the goal. Rich dived for the ball.

The crowd screamed.

Whistles screeched.

A Colton player tried to reach the bad pass. He sprinted forward, careening into Rich and sending them both sprawling onto the field.

Barri was on her feet as the players untangled themselves. The Colton player stood, but Rich writhed on the ground, holding his knee.

"Oh, no!" Barri cried, starting toward the field.

Melanie's hand curled around Barri's arm. "You can't go down there!"

"He's hurt!"

All the players surrounded Rich. Coach Morris and the team manager ran onto the field, while the referees tried to calm Rich's teammates.

Barri's stomach wrenched. What if Rich was really hurt badly?

The Colton Cougars returned to the bench, as did the rest of the Eagles. But Rich was still lying on the field, his face white, his mouth tight at the corners. Coach Morris bent on one knee and, talking all the while, examined his leg.

Barri held her breath.

"He'll be all right," Melanie said, but she didn't

sound convinced. The crowd in the stands began to whisper and speculate about the seriousness of the injury.

"Might be a sprained ankle."

"Or worse. Did you see how he went down? My guess is a break."

Barri felt sick.

Gingerly, and with the help of the coach, Rich struggled to his feet. Coach Morris motioned for two players from the bench to help Rich off the field, then signaled the second-string goalie to take Rich's place.

"Oh, no," Barri whispered. Her insides shaking, she couldn't take her eyes off Rich. He was pale and winced whenever his right foot touched the ground. "His leg—"

"Look, it's not broken or anything," Melanie whispered. "Otherwise he would be on a stretcher."

Barri shot Melanie a murderous glance. "That's encouraging."

"Well, it is!"

"I hope so," Barri worried aloud, as Rich, benched, held an ice pack to his thigh.

From then on, the game was over. The second-string goalie didn't have a chance, and the rest of the team seemed to wilt. The final score was the Colton Cougars seven—the Eagles four. "I've got to talk to Rich," Barri said to Melanie as the crowd and the team began to disperse. Working her way through the throng, Barri finally reached the players' bench. Rich, encumbered by crutches, was struggling with his athletic bag. His pale face split into a wide grin at the sight of her.

"What happened?" she asked, throwing her arms around him and nearly knocking him over again.

"Hey, slow down," he said, but his strong arms surrounded her and she felt better. "I just got knocked down."

"And . . . "

"And we think he pulled a thigh muscle," the coach replied.

"Is that bad?"

Rich's face clouded, and he muttered angrily, "Bad enough to keep me off the field for a couple of weeks."

Barri understood how disappointed Rich was. She would be angry and disappointed if an injury kept her sidelined from a major Fillmore production. "But—you'll be okay?"

"I should be."

"I still want a doctor to look at him," Coach Morris said. "Come on, Rich."

"I'll call you later," Rich said, releasing her grudgingly.

"Right." Barri waved, watching as Rich hobbled over to the coach's truck.

"Don't worry about him," Melanie advised later as she drove Barri home. "He's tough. He'll be all right."

"I hope so," Barri said.

"Besides, if you want to worry, why don't you concentrate on the audition next week? Now *that's* something to be concerned about."

"I don't need anything else," Barri said emphatically. Between Rich's injury and Joel's bad mood, she had enough worries to last her a lifetime!

CHAPTER EIGHT

"AUNT Laura!" In stocking feet Barri bounded down the last two stairs, then slid on the polished hardwood of the foyer.

Her aunt, Laura Layton, breezed in the front door, looking *absolutely* like a TV star! Aunt Laura's black hair swept her shoulders, her green eyes twinkled, and her wide lips curved into a smile.

"I've been trying to call you," Barri said.

"And I've been out of town," Laura replied with a wink. "We were filming on location for the sweeps."

Mrs. Gillette, who had opened the door, hugged her younger sister. "What're you doing here?"

"I thought I'd surprise you," Barri's aunt replied.

"Well, you did. And look at you," Mrs. Gillette marveled. "You look great!"

"Where were you on location?" Barri demanded.

"The Bahamas," Laura replied.

"Oh, I would've died and gone to heaven," Barri exclaimed. "The Bahamas!" Everything her aunt did was exciting. "Tomorrow Is Another Day" was the best soap opera on daytime television!

"Believe me, it was a lot of work," her aunt said, shrugging out of her sweater jacket and slinging it onto a hook on the brass hall tree. "Oh, Celia, what're you doing now?" she asked, eyeing the bare banister and unvarnished steps.

"Everything. From top to bottom. Come into the kitchen. I'll make some coffee and fill you in."

"I'll be there in just a second." Laura turned to Barri. "What was it you were calling me about?"

For a second Barri wanted to confide in her aunt about the contest she'd entered, but she held her tongue. If and when she was selected to audition for a part on the soap, she'd surprise Aunt Laura by strolling onto the set of "Tomorrow Is Another Day" as one of the extras. "I called because I thought you'd want to know I got the lead in the school play."

"You did? The lead?" Aunt Laura's eyes danced, and she hugged Barri fiercely. "Oh, honey, that's great!" When Barri didn't respond, Aunt Laura held her at arm's length. "It is great, isn't it?"

"Yes and no," Barri admitted as they walked into the kitchen. The coffee maker was already gurgling, and the scent of mocha filled the room. As quickly as possible Barri explained her predicament.

"So you see," Barri's mother finished, pouring three cups of mocha, "Barri's put herself between the rock and hard spot."

Laura blew across her steaming mug. "Better to have too much work than not enough."

"But I might lose all my friends."

"This Joel, just what kind of a friend is he?" Laura asked. "Doesn't he know how much trying out for Juliet means to you?"

"He's not seeing it from my angle," Barri admitted as the phone rang.

"I'll get it!" Before Mrs. Gillette could reach the phone, Jeff hurtled through the room like a hurricane. "It's for me," he pronounced before answering. "Hello ... Oh, yeah, she's here." Frowning so deeply that lines creased his freckled forehead, he handed the receiver to Barri. "It's Rich," he said in a singsong voice.

Barri snatched the phone from his hand. "Hi!" she said, twisting the cord and turning away from Jeff, who was pointing at his watch and mouthing for her to hurry up.

"Hi." Rich sounded down. "I'm sorry I didn't call sooner, but I just got back from the hospital."

Barri's heart dropped to her stomach. "Hospital?"

"The coach insisted on X rays, but everything checked out. All I've got is a pulled thigh muscle."

Relieved, Barri said, "I'm glad it's not worse."

"Yeah, but it's not good," Rich grumbled. "I'll miss the next couple of games, maybe more."

"It'll be okay," she consoled.

"Easy for you to say," he growled.

"You're not in a cast or anything, are you?" Barri asked.

"No, but—"

"Then we can still go out. Right?"

Rich actually chuckled. "I guess so—as long as it's not dancing."

"The next dance isn't for three weeks," she pointed out.

"Right, and by then, you'll be tied up in rehearsals."

Barri felt a little self-conscious. She glanced over her shoulder, but Jeff had vanished, and her mother and Aunt Laura were huddled over their cups at the table, talking rapidly and paying no attention to her whatsoever. "I've always got time for you," she whispered.

"I'll remember that."

They talked a little longer until Jeff sauntered into the room. Frowning and jabbing a finger at the digital clock over the microwave oven, he nudged Barri.

"Okay, okay," she mouthed before saying goodbye to Rich and hanging up. Whirling on Jeff, she demanded. "What're you waiting for?"

"Billy Ross! He's got a real old baseball card of Mickey Mantle, and he wants to sell it to me!"

"Hey, whoa!" Celia said, catching the end of the conversation. "Talk to me before you do any major league trading, okay? You still owe me your allowance."

Jeff rolled his eyes. "But that was a long time ago."

"A deal's a deal!" his mother reminded him.

Laura motioned Barri over to the table. "Tell me all about *Thin Ice* and Jamie Winston. Then, maybe we can rehearse your lines together."

"Would you?" Barri asked, delighted.

"Absolutely!"

Celia winked at her sister as she poured them each a second cup. "But first, while Laura and I catch up, Barri, you can finish your other homework."

"Oh, Mom—" Barri began to protest, but caught the meaningful gleam in her mother's eye. "Okay, okay. I'll be done in half an hour!" With that she dashed up the stairs.

Two hours later, Barri and Aunt Laura were in her room, drinking diet soda and studying Joel's script. Barri had changed into her best gray slacks, black vest, and red blouse, hoping to feel more the part of Jamie through her wardrobe. She'd even added her mother's expensive earrings and bracelet and pinned her hair jauntily over one ear, thinking that if she looked like Jamie, she would be Jamie. "You know," Aunt Laura said, skimming the final scene, "this is a wonderful play. It's funny and dramatic and nearly brings tears to my eyes. Joel's talented."

"So I've heard," Barri mumbled, feeling a little contrite. "And if it weren't for *Romeo and Juliet*—"

"I understand." Laura stretched out on Barri's bed and propped her chin in her palm. "I guess you shouldn't worry too much. Either way you win."

"What do you mean?"

"If you're cast as Juliet, you'll be on cloud nine, and if you don't, well, you're still the lead in *Thin Ice*. You can't lose."

"I suppose not," Barri admitted, not completely sure.

"Of course not. Joel will handle it. This is all part of the business, you know."

"Is it?"

"Oh, sure. Of course, where there are contracts involved, it's a little stickier. That's where the agents come in—to untangle all the legal mess. But I've been in stage productions where the lead actor gets an offer of a prime-time series or a part in a movie. Things have to be worked out. Sometimes, depending upon the contract, you can renegotiate your deal; other times, if the contract is ironclad and the producers won't work things out, you're stuck."

Barri hugged her knees to her chest. "It all sounds so exciting!" she said.

Aunt Laura laughed. "Sometimes it is, and other times it's just a job."

"No way!" Barri said, shaking her short dark curls emphatically. "Acting is always the greatest!"

"I hope you'll always think so," Aunt Laura said as she stood and yawned. "I'd better head back to New York. It's getting late."

"Can't you stay over?" Barri pleaded.

"Next time," Aunt Laura promised. "When I come up to see you—as Juliet or Jamie."

"Okay, people, listen up!" Mr. Heifetz said after school on Monday. The cast and crew for *Thin Ice* were assembled in the drama department's Green Room, which was just an old classroom next to the auditorium that the Thespians had painted green and decorated with props. "Let's talk about how we're going to run this production; then we'll do a read-through. Does everyone have a script?"

A timid girl in the second row raised her hand. "I—I don't."

"Here." Mr. Heifetz handed her an extra copy and the girl, Melissa Heffernon, blushed to the roots of her strawberry-blond hair.

Oh, great, Barri thought, wondering how anyone so shy could possibly perform in front of a live audience.

"Now, I expect the actors to study their characters—get into the characters' heads. Know what motivates your character. Some of you have been onstage before—I'll expect you to help the new people.

"We only have a few weeks of rehearsal, and believe me, it won't be enough. The first week we'll work in here while the set is being built. Then we'll block the play and start rehearsals onstage next week. So, be thinking not only about what your character is saying, but also, what he's *doing*."

Mr. Heifetz looked over the tops of his wire-rims to Joel, seated near the back of the room. "By the time we start blocking on the stage, Joel will have the props organized, the prompt book complete, and he'll mark all your cues." He looked around the room at about twenty totally unanimated actors and technicians. "Any questions?"

Barri bit her lip. She felt Joel's eyes boring into her back. Now was the time she should come clean and tell Mr. Heifetz about *Romeo and Juliet*. Sweat beaded her brow.

"What about costumes?" a girl behind Barri asked.

Barri let out a long sigh.

"We're working on them. The Thespians and home ec department are working together. If any of you have anything in your closets or your parents' closets that you'd like to donate," he said, opening his hands, "we'll take just about anything."

"That goes for props, too," Joel added.

"The Thespians will start a major drive next week. Now, any other questions?"

When no one raised a hand, Mr. Heifetz asked the actors to move their chairs into a circle and begin reading their lines. Unfortunately, Joel's chair was situated directly across from Barri's. Even though his eyes were shaded by aviator sunglasses, Barri knew he was staring at her.

"Okay—we're at the Winston home in Act One, right? Remember, this is a huge, beautiful house—a mansion that the Winstons have recently purchased. Their daughter, Jamie, who's been away at a private school and has to face the fact that she may be flunking out, has come home to tell her parents. She has a history of fantasizing, and now, before she can break the news about flunking out to her mother and father, she thinks she spies a ghost. Her family doesn't believe her, of course, and they think she might be going insane." Mr. Heifetz glanced around the room.

Barri followed his gaze. Half the actors were staring out the window, two were listening raptly to Mr. Heifetz, and the timid strawberry-blond girl,

Melissa, couldn't take her eyes off Joel. She has a crush on him, Barri realized, groaning inwardly.

"Okay. The first line is yours, Barri."

Barri glanced down at the script and started reading, but no matter how hard she tried to get into the part of Jamie, she felt wooden and dull. And the rest of the cast was worse. The boy who played Jamie's brother, Peter, continually lost his place and Melissa stumbled over her lines.

During the read-through, Joel's expression remained completely blank except for two deep furrows wedged between his eyes. Barri knew he was trying desperately not to show how upset he was.

She didn't feel any better. In fact, Barri felt sick. She tried to get into the part of Jamie, but her thoughts went ahead to that night and auditioning for the part of Juliet.

"All right, that's enough for today," Mr. Heifetz finally said, eyeing the group dubiously. "Start memorizing—I hate that word.—"He motioned nervously with one hand. "Start learning your part and understanding it; then the character will come alive within you, and you'll say your lines naturally. Don't concentrate on acting, but _become_ your character. We'll do another read-through tomorrow."

Barri gathered her script and books and saw Joel, army jacket tossed over his arm, stride out of the room. "Joel, wait!" She caught up with him in the hallway near the front doors.

"What?" he asked, then let out a weary sigh. "Did you see what happened in there?" he asked, yanking off his glasses and rolling his eyes. "It was a disaster! A bloody disaster!"

"It—it wasn't so bad."

"Not bad?" he repeated, looking at her as if she'd lost her mind. "Not bad?"

"It was only the first run-through. . . ."

"But it stank!" He flung one hand up in the air. "The best play I've ever written, and it's going to die—*die*—in front of the whole town!"

"You don't know that."

Leaning one shoulder against a bank of lockers, he smiled grimly. "No, I suppose I don't. I don't even know if you're going to be there or not, do I?"

Barri swallowed hard. "Not until later this week."

"Well, that's just great, Barri. Real great. Don't let the fact that my reputation as a playwright is on the line bother you, okay? It's no skin off your nose!"

"That's not fair!"

"Isn't it? Maybe not, but think about what you're doing! How fair is that?" He started out the door, turned, and looked over his shoulder, then, scowling, strode outside.

Barri, clinging to her books, sank against the lockers. Hot, fat tears stung her eyes.

"Are you okay?" Melanie asked, appearing from around the corner.

"I—I thought you'd already taken off."

"I had, but"—Melanie shrugged—"I wanted to know how it went."

Barri sniffed. "Did you hear what Joel said?"

"Most of it."

"Well, he's right. I'm afraid *Thin Ice* is going to be the worst disaster that's ever hit Fillmore High!"

"It couldn't be that bad."

"You wouldn't believe it."

Melanie blew her bangs out of her eyes. "Come on, I'll give you a ride home. We don't have long, you know. Tonight's the night!"

Barri, though she still was wounded, couldn't help but feel a tingle of anticipation. Her heart began to pound. Melanie was right. That night they would get to meet Ward McKenna and also have a chance to work with him.

"Let's go," she said, her worries disappearing. Right now, despite Joel and *Thin Ice,* she planned on throwing herself into the role of Juliet Capulet!

CHAPTER
NINE

"MOM, you didn't!" Barri exclaimed, hardly believing her eyes. Standing in front of her dresser mirror, where she and Melanie had been furiously primping, Barri opened the bag from The Fashion Connection and withdrew the silver shoes, purse, and belt. Another smaller package held the white enamel bracelet with painted silver-and-gold slashes and a pair of matching earrings.

Celia Gillette chuckled. "Melanie told me how much you wanted them. Consider it an early birthday gift."

Barri threw her arms around her mother. "You're the greatest!"

"Thanks. Now, you go 'knock 'em dead,' or is it 'break a leg'?"

"Both! And we intend to!" Melanie promised.

Barri put on a magenta silk blouse and tapered black skirt, then added the silver accessories. She felt a little guilty because she looked more like Jamie Winston than Juliet Capulet, but she didn't have time to second-guess herself.

"Perfect!" Melanie insisted as she eyed her

friend. Dressed in her coppery jumpsuit, her blond hair swept over one ear, Melanie looked sensational. "Come on, we don't want to be late!"

"See you later, Mom," Barri called as she and Melanie dashed down the stairs.

By the time Melanie parked in the lot of The Playhouse, a huge crowd had gathered. Would-be actors, set designers, lighting technicians, and costume coordinators whispered in the large, barnlike theater. Ward McKenna's name buzzed around the room, and necks craned whenever a rumor that he was already in the auditorium circulated.

"I don't know if I can stand this," Melanie admitted, her cheeks flushed, her eyes scanning the crowd as she and Barri slid into two vacant seats next to Geraldine.

"Me, neither." Barri's stomach was suddenly filled with butterflies.

"Shh—you'll do great!" Geraldine predicted as a tall, thin man with narrow features, thick black mustache, and receding hairline walked onto the stage. Wearing white Nikes, worn jeans, a blue work shirt and tweed jacket, he was, Barri guessed, either an actor or director.

She swallowed nervously.

He spoke into the microphone. "Hi, everyone, I'm Neal Larson," he began. "If you don't know already, I've agreed to direct *Romeo and Juliet*."

"He's a personal friend of Ward McKenna's parents," Geraldine whispered. "That's how he managed to get Ward to come back here to Merion."

The audience quieted. "I'm glad you're all here, and I think we should break into small groups.

Those of you who are auditioning for a part, stay here. Anyone who wants to work behind the scenes should see Francis Childers. . . . Frankie, where are you?"

"Over here, Neal," she called.

Shielding his eyes against the stage lights, he located a woman standing in the aisle near the back entrance. "Right—all the behind-the-scenes people, go with Frankie right now. The rest of you, take a seat in the few front rows. I'll call you as the parts come up. This is going to take quite a while, so I hope you plan on sticking around."

The crowd started shifting. Geraldine headed for the aisle, where Francis Childers was herding a small group, while Melanie and Barri moved up to the second row. They found seats near Robert and Kurt. Robert shifted nervously in his chair, and for once, Kurt had abandoned his Walkman and was paying rapt attention to the director.

"Okay—we'll try out the female parts first," Neal Larson said, grinning at the collective groan that went up. "See, ladies, chivalry isn't dead yet."

"Give me a break," Robert murmured under his breath.

Mr. Larson continued. "Most of you—well, probably all of you—know that the part of Romeo is being played by Ward McKenna. Ward, come up here."

From the back of the theater, Ward walked swiftly to the stage. All eyes turned to him, and Barri heard Melanie gasp as the stage lights caught his thick black hair. He turned, his blue eyes striking against his California-tan skin. He was about five nine or ten, his smile disarming, a huge dimple creasing his right cheek.

The crowd applauded, a few of the boys hooted, and Ward flashed his famous off-center smile.

Barri's heart flipped over.

Mr. Larson held up his hands. "Ward's agreed to audition with you, so let's get started. I'll read any of the extra parts. I expect each of you to read from the script."

As Mr. Larson instructed everyone, Barri's eyes never left Ward. She'd expected him not to look as good as he did on television. But she was wrong. He was more handsome than she'd ever dreamed possible. His jaw was strong, his build lanky, his smile dazzling.

Melanie was positively melting next to Barri. "This is just *too* wonderful!" she said with a heartfelt sigh.

"Carter, Megan!" Mr. Larson called, and a petite blond girl, her eyes bright, her cheeks rosy, climbed onto the stage. "Okay, tell Ward what scene you're auditioning with; then, when you're ready, you can start."

The girl, obviously star struck at being so close to Ward McKenna, had trouble pointing out the right page, but then she began reciting lines from act three, scene five, set in Juliet's chamber: " 'Wilt thou be gone? It is not yet near day. It was the nightingale and not the lark . . .' "

Barri watched as each of the girls auditioned. Some were good, others fair, and a few were exceptional.

Ward McKenna didn't miss a beat. He obviously

knew the play by heart and managed to become Romeo, acting as if he loved each and every girl who auditioned with him. Both Barri and Melanie sat transfixed for the next hour and a half.

"Gillette, Barri," Mr. Larson called as a pretty but slightly mush-mouthed would-be Juliet exited stage left. Barri froze. Her heart jumped to her throat, and her feet wouldn't move. She broke out in a cold sweat between her shoulder blades.

Melanie nudged her. "Go!"

Scrambling to her feet, Barri headed for the stage and wished she'd never agreed to audition. Ward was waiting, his smile a little worn around the edges, as she fumbled with the script, pointing out the death scene.

He was more handsome up close, Barri realized, hoping she didn't look as lovesick as some of the other actresses.

"I guess I don't have to worry about fouling up my lines," Ward said, as if amused, as he lay across the stage.

"Okay, let's go," Mr. Larson said. "Start with Juliet waking up. I'll be the friar."

Barri lay on the stage and tried to concentrate. Slowly, she roused herself, as if she were still half-asleep. " 'O comfortable Friar, where is my lord? I do remember well where I should be . . .' "

She felt herself become Juliet and saw the love of her life dead by his own hand. Speaking Shakespeare's verse, she fell to her knees, pretended to find a cup clasped in Ward McKenna's hand, and when that cup was empty, she held her breath and brushed her lips over Ward's mouth. He didn't stir, but a flood of excitement swept through her, and she could barely say the next words. Hoping she seemed stricken over Romeo's death, she pretended to snatch a dagger from Romeo and then sheathed the invisible knife in her abdomen. She fell across Ward's body, felt his muscles tense, and then lay still.

A few seconds later, Mr. Larson said, "Thanks, Ms. Gillette. Next. Todd, Melanie."

Barri struggled to her feet and, wondering if her performance had been authentic, exited stage left.

"Great job," Melanie whispered as they passed on the stairs backstage.

"Good luck."

Barri had just slid into her seat when Melanie pointed out the balcony scene to Ward, then began acting out her interpretation of Juliet Capulet.

Barri watched in fascination. Melanie was flawless. As the love-struck Juliet, she whispered her lines to an invisible Italian sun, then cast worshipful eyes on Romeo. Barri couldn't help but wonder if Juliet were speaking to Romeo, or Melanie to Ward. It didn't really matter. Melanie was captivating, to the point that she actually outshined Ward's Romeo.

With a sinking heart Barri knew she'd lost the part to Melanie. No one could top her performance.

"Thank you, Ms. Todd," Mr. Larson said, and Barri saw a smile twitch under his thick mustache.

"You were sensational," Barri whispered to Melanie when she returned.

"Oh, I hope so." Melanie's eyes were bright, her

color high, and an energy radiated from her every pore.

"You were good enough to make me sick," Barri said, feeling more than a little twinge of envy.

"Knock it off."

"I'm serious! If you don't get the part, I'll want to know why!"

They watched the rest of the auditions. After several hours Robert and Kurt tried out for the parts of Mercutio and Tybalt, each acting so well, Barri was sure they'd win the roles and end up fencing with each other on the stage.

By the time they left the theater, Melanie's feet were still several inches off the ground. "I didn't think it was possible," she said as she and Barri climbed into her Mustang, "but Ward's even better-looking in person."

"I thought so, too."

"Oh, I just hope I get the part," Melanie said, squeezing her eyes shut as if she were sending up a quick prayer. "I'll just *die* if I don't get to work with him."

Barri couldn't help but smile. "And you'll just die if you do," she quipped, remembering the death scene.

"Oh, you know what I mean," Melanie replied with a giggle. She switched on the engine, adjusted the radio, and as a throbbing rock song blared through the speakers, drove Barri home.

"I got a callback!" Melanie's voice cracked in her excitement. She stood on the front porch of Barri's home, her face aglow, her soaring spirits dancing in her blue eyes. Melanie Todd was on cloud eighteen and still climbing!

Barri had trouble finding her voice. She stepped out of the way so that Melanie could come inside. "You did—you mean for *Romeo and Juliet*?"

"Yes!" Melanie's smile just wouldn't quit. "Did you?"

"No—er, not yet."

"Oh." Her grin slipped a little. "Maybe they haven't called everyone yet."

"When did they call you?" Barri closed the door, bracing herself. She knew deep down that no one from the theater had tried to phone her. No one was going to.

"This morning! I called you, but the phone was busy."

Barri tried to put some enthusiasm in her voice. "Mom's working on a new project. She's been on the phone for hours."

"So, maybe Mr. Larson tried to call you and couldn't get through!" Melanie suggested.

"Maybe," Barri said, walking with Melanie into the kitchen. She opened the refrigerator door, extracted a couple bottles of diet root beer, and didn't believe for a minute that someone from the theater had tried to get through. No, she hadn't won the part. It was just that simple. She poured the root beer into glasses filled with ice. "Here's to your success!" she said, clinking her glass against Melanie's.

"And yours," Melanie said.

"I won't get the part." Barri couldn't hide the defeat in her voice.

"You don't know that, and besides, you're still Jamie Winston, aren't you?"

Barri smiled inwardly as she thought about Aunt Laura's words: *Either way you win!*

"I guess you're right," Barri whispered, hoisting her glass in mock salute. "Here's to Jamie Winston and Juliet Capulet."

"Let's hope," Melanie agreed. "But keep your fingers crossed. So far it's just a callback."

"You'll get the part," Barri predicted, her expression certain. "Just give another performance like you did last Monday."

"I'll try," Melanie said, dropping into one of the chairs at the kitchen table. Felicia, who had occupied that very chair, hopped to the floor and cast Melanie a suspicious glance. "So, tell me about *Thin Ice.*"

"Don't even ask," Barri warned. "It's worse than even Joel expected. Most of the cast can't act at all!"

"You're exaggerating!" Melanie sipped from her glass.

"Not really. We've read through the script for the last five days, and Monday we start blocking onstage. I only hope things improve," Barri said, remembering back to the read-throughs and shuddering. "Joel's sure *Thin Ice* will be the only play in Fillmore's history to close on opening night."

"That's crazy."

"You'd think so. But unless some of those kids can act better than they read, we're in trouble. Big trouble."

"Things'll get better."

"They have to," Barri agreed, tossing her dark curls out of her face and staring into her glass. "One of the girls, Melissa, is really nervous. She's always stammering and goofing up. I told her I'd go over her lines with her."

"Melissa?"

"She's a freshman," Barri explained. "And I think she's in love with Joel." Melanie's blond eyebrows inched up in interest.

"And Joel?"

"Doesn't know she exists. But then, Joel wouldn't see a stampeding rhino if it were charging down Fillmore's hallowed halls right now. He's so worried about *Thin Ice*, he can't think of anything else."

"Should he be?" Melanie asked. For the first time in weeks she seemed genuinely concerned.

"Oh, yeah," Barri thought aloud. "He should be worried. Very worried."

CHAPTER TEN

"GIVE me five!" Robert shouted to Kurt. They'd run into each other in the hallway near the gym.

Kurt, grinning ear to ear, bopping his head in time with his Walkman, slapped Robert's hand and hooted.

Barri smiled wistfully.

"You should've gotten a part, too," Rich said, still hobbling on crutches. "You know, you're the best actress in the entire school!"

"I think maybe you're prejudiced."

"I'm no expert, but I've seen you act. That director at The Playhouse made a big mistake."

Barri shrugged. "It's okay. Besides, Melanie's had more experience with tragedy."

"Melanie? Miss Got-Bucks?"

"I mean on the stage." Barri punched him in the arm but couldn't help grinning. Sometimes Rich could lift her up when she was feeling low. In his own way he understood.

Melanie, blond hair flying, sprinted down the hall. "Did you hear? Did you?" she cried, her face aglow. "*I* got the part! *I* get to be Ward McKenna's

Juliet!" She hugged herself as if she still couldn't believe it was true. "I didn't know what to think," she admitted. "Everyone at the callback was *so* good."

"You were the best," Barri said. She'd gone with Melanie and watched as Melanie, Kurt, and Robert had tried out against a handful of kids who were called back. Once again, Melanie had been brilliant. "I'm not surprised."

"I couldn't have done it without you!" Melanie enthused. "Thanks for going with me."

"Anytime." Barri forced a cheery smile that felt a little fake. She couldn't help feeling a twinge of jealousy that Melanie was going to work with Ward McKenna. But part of acting was trying out and losing roles. The crummy part.

The bell rang, signaling the start of school, and Melanie, her feet barely touching the ground, took off.

"You'd better get to class," Barri said, glancing up at Rich.

"I'll walk you."

"You mean, you'll *limp* me, don't you?" she teased.

"Very funny, Gillette."

"Really, I can make it alone." She started down the hall, but Rich's hand dropped on her shoulder.

"Hold on a minute. I do know how you feel, you know."

"Oh?"

"It couldn't be much worse than how I feel about missing out on the next few games."

"It's not quite the same," she said dryly. Honestly, comparing a couple of soccer games to the chance of a lifetime, working with a prime-time television star!

"Not so different. Think about it." Rich hobbled toward the gym.

Barri, lips clamped together, headed toward her first-period class. She tried not to think about *Romeo and Juliet*, but it seemed to be on everyone's tongue. All of the Thespians, except herself and Joel, were part of the cast or crew at The Playhouse, and Barri felt a little left out. As far as the production of *Thin Ice* was concerned, it was shaping into a disaster. The actors and technicians for Fillmore's production were the leftovers, the kids who couldn't make it at the local theater.

Maybe things will get better, she told herself. Starting this week, the rehearsals for *Thin Ice* would move to the auditorium, there would be room to move, people would find their marks, some of the nervousness of the new actors would fade. . . . "And you'll sprout wings and a tail," she told herself as she twirled the combination of her locker, withdrew her Spanish book, and glanced at the image of Michael J. Fox on the inside of her locker door. Was it her imagination, or did Michael look as if he were laughing at her?

"Some friend you are," she muttered, slamming the locker shut and telling herself to forget about *Thin Ice* until this afternoon, when, like it or not, she had to deal with all the problems of production.

* * *

"Not the big spotlight—the baby spot!" Joel yelled to the boy controlling the lights. "I think it's on the left of the dimmer board." Standing down-stage, his face tilted upward, his sunglasses thrust back on his head, he squinted at the overhead lights. First one, then another light was dimmed, until the boy running the dimmer board finally located the right combination. "That's it!" Joel said, then, muttering under his breath to Barri, added, "I think the guy's blind!" He strode over to the control panel to write the combination in the prompt book.

Barri walked around the stage. It was bare except for a few pieces of furniture and the skeleton of the set. She tried to imagine the stage being transformed into Jamie Winston's elegant living room. By opening night there would be a fireplace, long narrow windows, bookcase, coffee table. . . .

"Okay, now remember," Joel was saying to the boy in charge of the lights, "I want dry ice and gel every time Jamie thinks she sees an apparition."

"Gel?"

Joel's jaw tightened. "Right. Gel. The color filter for the light—remember?"

"Oh, yeah." The boy blushed. "What color?"

"Blue—we'll try blue. If it's not effective and can't be seen in the last row of the audience, we'll go with green or orange." Joel scribbled a note to himself. "And you'd better check and see if the fan works and what speed we'll need. We don't want our ghost hiding back here or shooting across the stage before Jamie sees it."

"Got it," the boy said, offering Joel a tentative smile.

"Good." Joel clapped him on the back, but Barri could tell by Joel's expression that he wasn't convinced. She felt for him. As stage manager, he had his work cut out for him.

"So, do I dare ask, 'How's it going?' " she whispered, once they were out of earshot of the rest of the cast.

"Not if you want to live until tomorrow."

"That bad?"

"Worse."

"Come on—" she cajoled.

"All right," Mr. Heifetz called loudly. "Let's walk through this thing! From the top. The curtain opens, and Jamie enters."

Everyone scattered to the wings.

Barri, closing her eyes for a second, felt Jamie come to her. She thought about Jamie's news that she was flunking out of school and the fact that she'd have to confront her parents. Her step faltered a little, and her voice betrayed her lack of confidence. "Mom? Dad?" she called, walking onto the stage, her head swinging toward the audience. "I'm home!" She paused, glanced around the room, and flopped onto the couch. "Where are they?" she wondered to the audience, tapping her fingers nervously on the arm of the couch.

"Jamie?" The shy girl who played Jamie's sister, Liz, flew into the room and slid across stage.

"Hold it right there!" Mr. Heifetz ordered. "Melissa, I like the fact that you're in character *before* you enter, but even though you're playing an energetic twelve-year-old, you have to be aware of the audience. Tone it down, and face the first row. Everyone out here, even in the worst seats, has to see you. Okay, you can scamper in, but remember, this isn't the hundred-meter dash, okay?"

Melissa nodded and bit her lip. "Okay," she murmured.

"All right—let's take it from your entrance again. Your cue was 'Where are they?'"

Barri cast a worried glance at Joel, who was seated in the middle of the auditorium, watching the action. Even though he sat in the dark, Barri could see him nervously biting his nails.

"Okay—here we go!" Mr. Heifetz clapped his hands and Melissa, as Liz, skipped into the room.

Barri groaned inwardly. She didn't know any twelve-year-old girls, especially tomboys, who skipped. Fortunately Mr. Heifetz didn't stop the action again, and Barri told herself that she'd read through everything with Melissa later—this time with action.

Barri and the rest of the cast made it through the walk-through in a little over three hours. During that time, Mr. Heifetz coached the new actors on how to enter and exit. "Always stay in character," he insisted. "Just because you've said your last line, doesn't mean you can shake off the character's mood. Keep that mood with you as you exit. Now, when you leave, don't turn your back on the audience, not even when you're going through one of the 'doors.' Watch me." He demonstrated, opening the door with his upstage hand, stepping through, and closing it with his other hand. "Be sure you're near the door before your exit, so there are no pauses on stage and the remaining actors can finish talking."

Running his hands through his frizzy hair, he eyed the cast. "That's about it for tonight," he said. "We still have a lot of work to do, but I think we've made some real progress. I'll see you tomorrow. Same time. Same place."

Barri tucked her script under her arm and started out of the auditorium.

"Hey, wait up!" Surprised, she turned to find Joel running down the aisle toward her. "Need a ride?" he asked, forcing a smile over his worried features. "I finally got my license last week, and Mom let me use the car."

"No, thanks, my mom said she'd be here—but it's great that you got your license."

"Yeah, now maybe I can pay Melanie back for all the rides she gave me."

"Right."

"And maybe after practice some night, we could go get something to eat down by The Playhouse. We could meet some of the kids down there."

"Sure," she said, "but I've really got to go." Barri turned, but he caught her arm.

"Hey, look, I'm sorry," Joel said, his jaw working. He wasn't very good with apologies. "I, uh, was a total jerk last week."

Barri rolled her eyes. "Maybe I was, too."

"I'm sorry that you didn't get the part of Juliet."

"Really?"

He grinned, flashing straight white teeth. "Well, no, not really. I'd rather have you playing Jamie, but I am sorry you didn't get something you wanted."

Shrugging, Barri pushed open the side door of the building. "It's okay," she said as they walked together down the concrete steps to a sidewalk that cut through a broad expanse of grass. A night breeze blew through the elm trees on the lawn, and a few dry leaves blew across the sidewalk.

Barri shivered.

"Cold?"

"Not really." She glanced at him. "You?"

"Nah. I'm fine."

"Just worried."

Joel's brows pinched together. "Wouldn't you be? My career's on the line here. I can read the reviews already: 'Joel Amberson, local playwright, peaks at sixteen, with the sloppy production of *Thin Ice*. Not only poorly cast, with the one exception of Ms. Barri Gillette, but also ineptly produced, *Thin Ice* will go down in the history of the Fillmore drama department as the biggest bomb ever!' "

"It's not that bad!"

Joel squinted up at the stars. "Not that bad," he repeated. "Barri, you're an eternal optimist."

"Well, look at it this way—it couldn't get any worse."

"I suppose you're right," Joel said.

Barri crossed her fingers. She didn't tell it to Joel, but she was afraid things could get much worse. What if no one remembered their lines? What if the scenery, already behind schedule, didn't get finished?

"There's my mom," she said, seeing Mrs. Gillette's bronze wagon pull around the corner. She dashed across the lawn and called over her shoulder, "See you tomorrow!"

"Right."

Unfortunately things did get worse. Lots worse. None of the costumes fit; some of the props were missing; the scenery was way behind schedule; Melissa, who played Liz, kept flubbing her lines; and Tim, a boy who was supposed to play Peter, became so tongue-tied every time he was on stage with Barri, the cast couldn't get through even the simplest scenes.

"I'm ruined!" Joel moaned, with only a week of rehearsal left before opening night. Seated in a booth at Prime-Time Pizza, he gorged himself on Canadian bacon, sausage, pepperoni, and onions.

"*Thin Ice* is going to work out!" Barri proclaimed, though she had serious doubts herself. "You just have to think positively."

"I am. I'm positive it's going to flop!"

"You're a lost cause," she teased.

"Don't I know it?"

Barri twirled her straw in her Diet Pepsi and glanced up to see Robert shoving open the door.

Right on his heels were Geraldine, Melanie, and Kurt.

Barri waved. Melanie spied Joel and Barri. "Over there," she said to the others.

"Hi!" Melanie practically fell into the booth, and her usual smile seemed to droop. "Jeez, I've had it!"

Kurt, Geraldine, and Robert didn't look much better.

"What's going on?" Barri asked, exchanging glances with Joel.

"It's Larson, the director," Robert groaned, flopping down in a nearby booth and rubbing the back of his neck. "He's a slave driver."

"And Ward McKenna," Kurt muttered, sitting beside him. "What a perfectionist!"

This was the first time either Barri or Joel had heard that things were less than rosy at The Playhouse.

"It's just because he's a star," Melanie defended, though her shoulders slumped a little.

A small smile played at the corners of Joel's mouth.

Frowning, Robert leaned over and grabbed a slice of Joel and Barri's pizza. "Did you know that *before* school, at six o'clock, the two gangs of Montagues and Capulets have an hour of dance and exercise class—then we practice fencing for another half hour?" He sighed. "By the time I run home, shower, and get to school, I'm exhausted."

"Don't forget the rehearsals every night!" Kurt complained.

Robert took a bite of pizza and swallowed quickly. "My parents don't know it, but I'm way behind in U.S. history and geometry."

Joel, his dark mood lifting, seemed about to say something, but Barri kicked him under the table. He barely flinched.

"What's that?" Geraldine said, making a face at the remaining pieces of pizza.

Joel grinned. "Protein, fat, complex carbohydrates—"

"Enough bad karma. I'll order us a vegetarian delight!"

Kurt and Robert exchanged worried glances. "No way," Robert said. "If we're paying for it, only *half* can be rabbit food; the rest has to be he-man stuff."

"He man stuff—how macho!" Geraldine shot him a killing look but didn't argue as he followed her to the counter to order. "So, how're things going with you guys?" Melanie asked.

Joel's expression turned dark again. "Just peachy," he muttered sarcastically.

Melanie bristled. "What's that supposed to mean?"

"Nothing!" Barri gave Joel an I'll-handle-this look. "We've got a couple of production problems, that's all."

"What kind?" Geraldine asked, plopping down with the playbill for order number forty-five.

"You name it," Joel muttered.

Geraldine's blue eyes shadowed a bit. "Costumes?"

"Costumes, lighting, scenery, props, publicity—"

"I get the picture," Geraldine said. "You know, I promised Mr. Heifetz I'd help, and I will."

"When?" Barri asked. "It sounds like you're already up to your eyeballs."

Geraldine eyed Barri and Joel's pizza as if she were about to give up vegetarianism and higher consciousness. "We can't let our famous playwright fall on his face, can we?"

Barri giggled.

Robert shrugged. "Sure, I'll help, too. I must have some time between midnight and six A.M. when I'm not too busy. Besides, who cares if I flunk U.S. history? Washington *was* the president during the Civil War, wasn't he?"

Everyone, even Melanie, laughed. "I don't know what I could do," she said.

"How about coaching?" Barri suggested.

"Melissa and Tim—" Joel groaned loudly, placing his hand over his heart. "Don't remind me."

"Do you think they'd want me to?" Melanie asked.

"It doesn't matter," Joel decided. "They don't have a choice."

"Then I'll do it," Melanie agreed as the next steaming pizza was placed on the table by the waiter.

Everyone grabbed a gooey piece, and Barri even tried a slice of the green pepper, mushroom, and onion. As far as pizza went, the vegetarian half left a lot to be desired, but Barri didn't really care. Finally the Thespians were pulling together again, working to salvage *Thin Ice*.

She only hoped it wasn't too late!

CHAPTER ELEVEN

"NO way!" Rich threw his head back and laughed. "Me? Paint scenery? You've got to be kidding!"

"Why not?" Barri demanded. "Everyone's helping out."

"They're all Thespians."

"You're sidelined from the soccer team, so you could be an honorary Thespian. Couldn't you just help us out by painting a windowsill or something?"

"Picasso I'm not!" Rich signaled to the waitress behind the counter at The Fifties.

"You don't have to be Picasso. All you have to do is slap some paint on a piece of cardboard or pound a nail into a brace for a backdrop. It won't be anything difficult, believe me."

Rich grinned, his dark eyes twinkling. "Promise?"

Barri held her right hand up, palm out. "On my honor!"

"Okay, okay," Rich agreed halfheartedly as a waitress in a pink checked dress and matching apron approached their table.

"What'll it be?" she asked.

"One all-American with a Cherry Coke—"

"Diet Cherry Coke," Barri interrupted. Though most of the food on the menu was realistic 1950s fare, the management had made a few concessions to the whims of more modern years. Diet soda was one of them.

"Right," Rich clarified, "a Diet Cherry Coke and a greaser with a double chocolate malt."

"You got it!" The waitress scratched on her pad, then moved to the next table before taking the tickets and tucking them into a spinning rack mounted over the counter.

"So you'll do it?" Barri asked, excited.

Rich grimaced. "I guess."

"Great. We're meeting at the theater at nine tomorrow morning!"

"Need a ride?"

"I'd love one!" Barri said, thinking how great Rich really was. With his dusty-blond hair, deep brown eyes, and barely visible freckles, he was an all-American himself. Though they sometimes fought, she really cared for him. The trouble was, she wasn't sure that she loved him. The waitress placed their order on the table, a cheeseburger and fries for Barri and a burger smothered in chili sauce—the greaser—for Rich.

"Just remember, Gillette," Rich said before he took a long swallow of his malt.

"What?"

"You owe me one."

* * *

"Okay, that should do it," Geraldine said, cocking her head to one side and eyeing her work. "Turn around." Barri did as she was asked, twirling in front of a tall, cracked mirror salvaged from a secondhand store several years before. It was now a permanent fixture in the girls' dressing room under the stage at Fillmore High.

"Is the hem straight?" Barri asked, surveying her appearance in the mirror. As Jamie Winston she went through three costume changes. Two of the outfits were her own, the last, a long cocktail dress, had been donated by Melanie's mother and had to be taken up to fit Barri.

"Mmm." Geraldine frowned as she studied the dress's hemline. Designed in pink silk with a small silver thread running through it, the gown draped over one shoulder, tucked in neatly at Barri's waist, then billowed to midcalf. "It's fine," Geraldine decided. "Now, what about the rest of your outfit—shoes, accessories, jewelry?"

Thinking of the silver pumps and accessories from The Fashion Connection, Barri grinned. "No problem."

"Good. That does it, then," Geraldine said with a weary smile. "I think all the costumes are set."

"Thanks a lot."

"Hey! We could use some help up here!" Kurt yelled from the stage above the dressing rooms. Hammers banged, scenery scraped overhead, and footsteps shook the low ceiling under the stage.

"Just when I thought I was going to make a quick exit," Geraldine muttered.

"We'll be there in a minute," Barri called back

before stepping out of the gown and changing into jeans and a sweatshirt.

The auditorium was a madhouse. Robert was taking charge of the lights and sound equipment, trying to explain to the sophomore boy in charge of the production how to work the control panel. Spot, flood, and beam lights flipped on and off rapidly, illuminating the stage, where workers from the vocational ed department as well as people involved with the play were constructing the set.

Music blared through the speakers while Kurt explained to Mr. Heifetz and Ms. Brookbank that the background music he taped would heighten the varying moods in *Thin Ice*. There was an eerie flute solo that Kurt had composed himself—it would be perfect for the appearance of the ghost on stage.

Mr. Heifetz and Joel were grinning; they obviously liked the music, but Ms. Brookbank's brows were pulled into an I-don't-see-how-this-can-possibly-help line.

"Hey! Grab a brush." Barri turned and found Rich, his bad leg propped on an ottoman from the Winston's living room, diligently painting posters for the hallways.

"I thought you were working on the set."

"I got promoted—or demoted, however you want to look at it."

The auditorium doors burst open, and Melanie, her hair pulled into a ponytail, breezed down the aisle. "I put posters up in the upper and lower halls at the school as well as three grocery stores, Parson's Pharmacy, The Shoe Rack, The Fashion Connection, The Fifties, Prime-Time Pizza, Los Tacos Locos, and Uncle Woo's Chinese Restaurant."

"Good." said Ms. Brookbank, who'd heard the tail end of the conversation. For once she wasn't in a prim suit or dress. That day she was wearing baggy overalls and her husband's work shirt. "Now, maybe you could work with Melissa, help her with her lines, and, Barri—" she swung her gaze in Barri's direction—"I really think you should go over your scenes with Tim. He seems positively terrified of you."

"Okay," Barri agreed.

"They're both waiting for you in the drama room."

"Terrified of me?" Barri repeated as Ms. Brookbank was called back to the discussion with Joel and Mr. Heifetz.

"Maybe dumbstruck is more appropriate," Melanie observed. "I've seen him watching you, Barri. I think he's interested."

Rich lifted a brow. "Uh-oh. Competition," he said.

"Give me a break," Barri muttered.

She and Melanie walked out of the auditorium. "So, how does it feel to be Merion's first Juliet?" Barri asked. One corner of Melanie's mouth curved up. "It's great, of course, and working with Ward"— she glanced up at the ceiling—"is heaven. But it's not exactly what I thought it would be."

"Meaning?"

"Oh, Barri, I'm in love with him!" Melanie blurted out, then bit her lip.

"In love?" Barri stopped dead in her tracks. "With Ward McKenna?"

Melanie nodded, swallowing hard. "I know it's crazy, but I can't help myself. We've been working together for nearly two weeks, and every time he kisses me or touches me, I just melt inside."

Barri couldn't believe her ears. She hadn't seen Melanie outside of school for the past week because they were both so busy with their productions. Melanie had gone with several boys in the past few years and had fallen in love with each of them—but this was different. Barri could sense it. "How does he feel?"

"Not the same," Melanie admitted nervously. "I think he likes me, but I can't really tell. He's *so* romantic onstage!" A small smile played on her lips.

"And offstage?"

The smile faltered. "He hasn't given me a second glance," Melanie admitted.

"Oh."

"Yeah, *oh*." Melanie sighed. "I've tried everything to get him to talk to me, but all he wants to do is work. He's such a perfectionist, we'll go over a line a zillion times, and he still won't be happy. And the director! Larson is a thousand times worse than Ms. Brookbank ever was. He's always shouting orders and getting mad. Sometimes I'm a nervous wreck *before* we get started."

Barri was thunderstruck. She'd expected everything on the set of *Romeo and Juliet* to be running smoothly. When things had been particularly bad with *Thin Ice*, she'd even regretted going out for the part of Jamie and wished she'd tried harder to land the part of Juliet or Lady Capulet.

"Everyone's nerves are shot," Melanie admitted, "but I wouldn't change anything for the world. Just being with Ward is *so* great."

"Have you talked to him—I mean, about other things besides the play?"

"I've tried. But he just clams up. I think he's one of those show business people who protect their privacy. It's not just me—he won't talk to anyone."

"A snob."

"No." Melanie shook her head emphatically. "I think he's one of those workaholics."

"Well, you've still got a couple of weeks," Barri said, her eyes gleaming. "No boy, not even Ward McKenna, can be immune to the Todd charm forever."

"I hope you're right."

Barri opened the door to the drama department and cringed. Melissa and Tim were already there, but instead of working on their lines, they were huddled over the latest copy of *Teen Idol*. They glanced up guiltily when the door opened.

"Ready to go to work?" Barri asked cheerfully.

"Sure!" Tim said, blushing.

But Melissa just stared at Melanie. "You play Juliet, right?" she asked.

"Uh-huh."

"Oh, how lucky! Ward McKenna's such a hunk!"

"He's a great guy."

"It's just too bad he's already engaged!" Melissa said.

Melanie gulped, and her face began to redden. "Engaged?"

"That's what it says here. That he and Jillian Donovan are engaged." Melissa whirled the magazine around on the desk top. A huge picture of Ward, his arm slung around the waist of a beautiful blond girl, covered one page. The two-column article, entitled "McKenna's Mysterious Leading Lady," filled the next several pages.

Melanie's face went from bright red to ashen as she scanned the article.

"Sometimes those magazines don't get the facts straight," Barri offered.

"Right. Well, it doesn't matter anyway," Melanie said shakily as she shoved the magazine back toward Melissa. "Now, don't we have some work to do?"

Barri slid into a chair next to Tim and wished she hadn't seen the tears collecting in the corners of Melanie's eyes.

The week didn't get much better. Melanie, though pretending to be over her infatuation with Ward McKenna, wasn't her usual self. Robert and Kurt acted as if they would die of exhaustion before opening night, and Joel's bad mood grew steadily worse.

Now, on Friday, as the final curtain fell on the dress rehearsal of *Thin Ice*, Barri heaved a tremendous sigh.

"Okay, people, that's it!" Mr. Hiefetz said to the actors who'd straggled back onstage.

Barri felt awful. Everything that could go wrong

had. Tim and Melissa had acted as if they'd never said their lines before, the lights had been fouled up, and the tape of Kurt's music had been garbled to the point that the eerie flute music sounded like a panicked flock of chickens. One part of the set had even fallen down when Tim had slammed a door too hard.

Joel, prompt book in hand, stalked onto the set. He pulled Mr. Heifetz aside and whispered, "We have to delay *Thin Ice*! No one's ready!"

Tight-faced, Mr. Heifetz deliberately avoided looking at Joel and concentrated on polishing his glasses. "The flyers have been out for a week, notices have been placed in the *Merion Observer* and the *Colton Tribune*. Posters are plastered all over town. We open tomorrow, Joel."

"But you saw—"

"No." Mr. Hiefetz settled his glasses on his nose. "This is all part of it. Sometimes things go well, other times they don't; but whatever happens, we have a performance to put on. Now, I expect everyone, including you, to give *Thin Ice* two hundred percent tomorrow night!"

Joel nodded, his mouth grim.

Barri mouthed, "Wait for me," then dashed downstairs to change out of her costume. Within minutes she was back in the auditorium and trying to cheer Joel out of his black mood.

"It'll be all right," she promised, pushing open the auditorium doors.

"I hope so," Joel murmured.

"Things'll change once there's an audience."

"Let's just hope they change for the better. I'll

see you tomorrow." Slinging his backpack over his
shoulders, he headed for the parking lot. And Barri,
watching him leave, wished she had a crystal ball.
What would really happen tomorrow night?

CHAPTER
TWELVE

BARRI stood in the wings, her stomach in knots. Breathe deeply, she told herself as she heard the rustle, coughs, and quiet whispers of the audience on the other side of the curtain.

Mr. Heifetz nodded to a boy on the other side of the stage. The house lights dimmed, and the curtain slowly rose. Joel, his tanned face pale, pointed at Barri.

Barri closed her eyes for just a second, then walked onto the stage. "Mom?" she called, glancing right and left, her worried face in full view of the audience. "Dad?" She bit her lower lip and said, "I'm home!"

Flopping onto the couch, she drummed her fingers on the overstuffed arm. "Where are they?" She paused, waiting for Melissa's entrance. When the girl didn't appear, she started to panic. The auditorium was quiet, and she was alone on stage. To avoid any dead time, she stood and called again, "Mom? Dad? I'm home!"

There was a thunder of footsteps, and Melissa, as Liz, flew across the stage, nearly toppling into

Barri. Her eyes were round, and when she realized Barri wasn't on the couch, she began to stammer. "J-Jamie—?"

"Hi! Boy, am I glad to see you," Barri said, cueing the girl as she sat again on the couch. "Where are Mom and Dad?"

"Mom and Dad?" Melissa said blankly, glancing nervously at Joel. She licked her lips. "Oh, they're out. Won't be back until six." Melissa found her mark and managed to mumble her lines without any of the emotion she and Barri had practiced for hours.

Barri's insides churned. She felt the character of Jamie slipping from her, and though she went through the motions and said Jamie's words, she was all too conscious of the audience, of the spotlight that didn't appear, of the lack of music, of the panic evident in Melissa's and Tim's eyes.

The first act went steadily downhill. No one remembered his cues, the houselights flickered twice, and one prop was missing. They faked it. Badly, but nonetheless, they muddled through the scene. Just before the curtain was lowered, Barri, alone on the stage, waited. The script called for her to have her first encounter with the ghost. Kurt's eerie flute music filled the auditorium. Barri turned and gasped just as a cloud of blue smoke entered the stage, only to disappear too quickly.

This isn't right, Barri thought wildly, realizing that half the audience hadn't seen the spirit that was supposed to linger on the stage long after Barri had made her exit.

The curtain came down with a thud, and Barri

let out her breath. "I'm doomed," Joel whispered as the audience clapped intermittently.

"Okay, okay!" Mr. Heifetz said, "Everyone change. The curtain goes up in ten! Let's pull this thing together!"

Worried that the play would surely flop, Barri dashed down the stairs to the dressing room. She yanked off her black skirt and white blouse, then slid into Melanie's mother's pink gown, only to hear a sickening rip as she inadvertently stepped on the hem. "Oh, please, no!"

Turning to view her rear in the mirror, she saw a huge gap in the back seam! The seam had ripped out from the bottom of the zipper to the hem. Pink silk parted, exposing the lace of her slip. "Oh, no!"

Tears welled in Barri's eyes, and she blinked hard as the other girls changed quickly. What could she do?

There was a tap at the door. "Barri? Can I come in?" Melanie poked her head into the room.

"Sure." Barri hardly looked up.

"Uh-oh," Melanie said, eyeing the dress. "Problems?"

"Just one more in a bucketful," Barri murmured.

"Hey, I can fix that!" Melissa, who had already changed, spied the rip in Barri's dress.

"How?"

"I didn't get an *A* in home ec for nothing." Melissa, unlike her usually shy self, found a needle and thread and started working furiously. "You just finish with your jewelry. And be careful. I only have time to baste this together."

There was a loud rap on the door. "Three minutes."

"There you go!" Melissa bit off the thread and slipped her feet into a pair of penny loafers.

Barri stepped into her pumps and clasped the enamel necklace around her neck.

"Hang in there," Melanie whispered.

"I don't know—"

"Sure you do! Come on, Barri! You're the star! This is your chance to show Merion what a great actress you are and what a wonderful play Joel's written."

"But you saw the first act!"

"Things can only improve." With a confident nod Melanie whisked out of the room.

"One minute, girls!"

Barri flew out of the room and up the stairs. She waited for the curtain to rise and entered, stage left. With a toss of her head, she became Jamie Winston.

Tim, as Peter, clomped onto the stage. He looked nervous and tongue-tied, but Barri gave him an encouraging wink and started her lines. To her amazement, her professionalism seemed to infect Tim as well as the rest of the cast.

The second act was a vast improvement over the first, and even the vanishing ghost stayed where it was supposed to.

"Okay, okay," Mr. Heifetz whispered when the curtain fell. "That's more like it. We can still pull this off. Tim—good job. Melissa, hang in there, you're doing great." His eyes landed on Barri and he winked. "Just keep doing what you're doing."

"I'll try," she whispered, looking past him to Joel, who was talking to the boy in charge of the lights and sound. Barri crossed her fingers, feeling as if the entire play and Joel's reputation balanced on her shoulders.

The curtain came up, and Barri transformed to Jamie Winston. She didn't act, she *was* a young socialite who had trouble in school and whose parents thought she was loosing her mind. Barri carried herself as Jamie, spoke through Jamie's voice, and even cried a few of Jamie's tears in the final scene.

By the time the curtain came down on act three, the crowd was applauding wildly. Barri and the rest of the cast linked hands and bowed before a filled auditorium, half of which was on its feet.

Heart pounding, eyes shining under the stage lights, Barri knew she'd just given the performance of her life. As she looked upon a sea of faces in the crowd, she saw Rich clapping madly, her parents beaming, Kelly grinning widely, and Jeff, with his fingers in his mouth, whistling! Aunt Laura was next to him, and she mouthed *Brava!* when she caught Barri's eye.

Backstage, Barri let out a sigh of relief and gasped when Joel grabbed her and spun her off her feet. "You did it, Gillette!" he said, grinning ear to ear. "I don't know how, but you really pulled it together."

"Give Melanie some credit."

"You mean Juliet, don't you?" he said sarcastically. Slowly he set Barri back on her feet.

"No, I mean Melanie! For your information, she

came into the dressing room after the first act, and she gave me a pep talk. And Melissa is the one who saved the day."

"Melissa?" Joel couldn't keep the skepticism from his voice.

"The best seamstress in the cast." Barri explained about the torn dress and Melissa's fast work under pressure.

Joel's brows rose by degrees. "Maybe Melissa should work with Geraldine from now on."

"That's not a bad idea." Barri started for the dressing room but stopped and grinned back at Joel. "Hey, Amberson," she said, her lips curving into a broad smile, "Congratulations."

"Thanks!" For the first time in nearly a month, Joel actually flashed his crooked smile. He flipped his aviator sunglasses onto his nose, though it was nearly eleven at night.

Barri felt better than she had in weeks. *Thin Ice* was going to be a success!

" '. . . and after a few false starts in the first act, *Thin Ice*, a play written by Merion's own Joel Amberson, was a delight. Barri Gillette, who played Jamie Winston, is a natural. Ms. Gillette gave a dazzling performance of the troubled socialite whose parents think she's losing her mind when she admits to seeing a ghost . . .' "

"I knew it!" Aunt Laura said as Barri read the rest of the review to herself. "Elizabeth Shue, move over!"

Barri laughed. "I don't think she has too much to worry about!"

"Not yet, maybe. But in a few years—" Aunt Laura leaned back in her chair and sipped from her coffee cup. Despite the fact that she, Barri, and Kelly had stayed up until nearly three the night before, Laura looked wonderful. Now, seated around the breakfast table, she and her nieces were waiting for Barri's parents to return from the River East Athletic Club.

"You really were great," Kelly said for about the sixtieth time since the end of act three. She glanced at her watch. "When do Mom and Dad usually get back?"

"Any minute. Mom's aerobics class is over at eleven."

The back door opened, then slammed shut. Jeff, followed by Bonecrusher, ran into the room. He flung his baseball cap onto the counter. "I'm hungry!" he announced, opening the refrigerator and hanging on the door.

"Wait till Mom and Dad get back."

"But I haven't had breakfast!"

Barri frowned. "What do you call two bagels with cream cheese?"

"A snack."

Aunt Laura laughed. "Well, if your folks are due back any minute, I'll start brunch." Rising, she glanced out the window. "Here they come now—oh!"

Bam! With a sickening thud of metal meeting metal, a loud crash resounded through the house.

"Oh, no!" Jeff's face turned white. "My bike!" He dashed through the back door.

Barri didn't move.

But Aunt Laura had trouble suppressing a smile. She looked at her two nieces. "I think the score is BMW one, BMX zip."

"I don't think we want to be here when Dad comes in," Barri whispered to her sister.

"Too late," Kelly replied.

Their father, the back of his neck dark red, his face grim, strode into the room. Jeff, looking absolutely dejected, was on his heels. "And that's the end of it. Until you can pay for the damage to the bike and the car, you're grounded."

"Dad!" Barri cried, then caught the glint in her father's eye.

"You have something to add?" he asked.

Taken aback, Barri couldn't help defending her brother. "It's just that he's only a little kid—"

"I'm not little!" Jeff said, fighting back tears.

"Good. You can prove it," their father said.

"Jack—" Celia put her hand on her husband's arm, and to Barri's surprise, he winked at her. This was an *act*? Dad wasn't really mad?

Jeff stomped up the stairs. Barri heard the door to his room slam before she eyed her father. "What's going on here?"

"I just want Jeff to learn some responsibility."

"And the car?"

Her mother grinned. "Not a scratch. The bike caught under the bumper."

Mr. Gillette smothered a smile. "It's hard to ruin the 'ultimate driving machine.' However, the BMX will need major repairs."

"Are you going to tell Jeff?"

"I'll give him about ten minutes to think things

over, then let him know the car's okay. But he will have to do chores around the house to fix his bike."

"And he still owes me," Celia Gillette added. "Now, how about brunch? I don't know about the rest of you, but I'm starved!"

"Me, too," Kelly said with a grin. "You should taste dorm food. *B.A.D.*"

After the crisis with Jeff had been put on hold and Aunt Laura had gone back to New York, Barri found Kelly sprawled across her bed, squinting at a biology book.

"I thought you needed a break from that."

"I do. But I've got a test next week." Kelly's eyes slitted in conspiration. "Can you keep a secret?"

"What do you think?"

"No, but I'll tell you anyway. The reason I'm a little behind in school—"

"Yeah?"

"His name is Josh."

Barri's mouth rounded. Kelly? A boyfriend? As far as Barri knew, her older sister hadn't dated anyone seriously since her sophomore year in high school. "Why didn't you say anything?"

"Because I just met him the day after school started. He's in my poly sci class."

"And—"

Kelly giggled, holding her book across her chest. "And I think I'm in love!"

"Oh, Kell, that's great!" Barri flung herself down on the bed. "So, spill it—every last, juicy detail. Where's he from? How'd you meet him? Does he have a younger brother?"

"Hey, slow down." Kelly laughed. "There's not much to tell. We've only dated a few times." Kelly went on about Josh, and her face absolutely glowed. Her cheeks turned rosy, her lips curved into a secretive smile, and her brown eyes danced. "He is *so* cute and so smart."

Barri had never known her sister to be so taken with a boy. Not since Peter Logan years before. "So what about you?" Kelly asked. "You're still going with Rich, right?"

Barri nodded.

"And—No one else?"

"No." Barri sighed and stared at the ceiling. "I like Rich a lot. I mean, *a lot*! But I don't know. . . . " Absently her fingers traced the stitching on her quilt as she tried to come up with the right words. "I just thought that when you fell in love, I mean, really in love, it would be different."

"How?"

"Rich and I fight a lot."

"And then make up?" Kelly asked, her dark brows rising.

"Yeah." Barri giggled. "But he's so . . . I don't know how to explain it."

"So much of a jock."

"I guess that's it. He doesn't understand how I feel about acting, not really. He can't believe that I'm really going to make it—that I'm going to be a star." She sighed theatrically, feeling a little like a tragic heroine herself. "Sometimes I just don't think we're made for each other."

"Then you probably aren't," Kelly agreed. "Don't

get me wrong, I like Rich, I think he's nice. But he just doesn't seem your type."

"My type?" Barri repeated. "And what's that?"

"Oh, I don't know. Someone with a little more flash—a little more dramatic flair. Someone like Joel Amberson."

"Joel!" Barri bolted upright on the bed. "Give me a break! Joel's an old friend, that's all."

"Okay, so not Joel. But someone who has the same interests you do, someone who can look into your soul."

"Oh, save me!" Barri tossed a pillow at Kelly and laughed, but deep inside, she wondered if Kelly was right.

The next two performances of *Thin Ice* went flawlessly. Joel, in a grand gesture, brought Barri roses on closing night. "Thanks, Barri," he said, handing her the bouquet of small pink buds. "You saved my life."

"No I didn't. *Thin Ice* would've been a success, with or without me."

He flashed his devilish smile. "We'll never know, will we?"

She giggled, then spied Rich waiting for her in the auditorium. "Are you going to see *Romeo and Juliet* next week?"

"Of course. This might be my only chance to see Ward McKenna in person," he cracked.

"Seriously."

Joel shrugged. "Sure, I'll go. I want to see Robert and Kurt slash each other to ribbons in the fight scene."

"Very funny," Barri mocked.

"You need a ride?"

"I don't know; it depends on Rich. If he wants to go—"

"Okay. I'll see you there." Snapping his shades over his eyes, Joel took off, and Barri fought her way through the throng to find Rich, who was frowning and shifting from foot to foot while he waited for her. "What was that all about?" he asked, eyeing the flowers.

"Joel's way of thanking me."

"Thanking you?"

"For doing such a good job."

"Oh."

She felt her dimple crease. "Kind of like a trophy."

"I get the picture," he said, but couldn't help watching Joel's back as he disappeared through a side door. "Come on, I thought we'd celebrate at Uncle Woo's."

"Sure." Barri threaded her arm through his and walked outside to the early-October night. A harvest moon hung low in the sky, and a slight breeze tickled her skin. She glanced up at Rich. He really was handsome. Moonlight caught in his pale hair, and his profile was strong. So why didn't she love him?

"You really were ... spectacular," Rich said, helping her into his pickup.

"Thanks." He slid in beside her. "And not to be outdone by Amberson ... " From beneath the seat, he pulled out a bouquet of roses, carnations, and baby's breath. "For you—Jamie Winston!"

"You didn't have to—"

"Shh." He placed a finger over her lips to silence her.

Barri's heart thundered, kicking into overdrive.

"I wanted to." Lowering his head, he kissed her. Barri melted as he wrapped his arms around her. She kissed him back and heard him groan. "You're the most gorgeous girl at Fillmore," he said, and Barri wondered why the compliment didn't touch her as it should have. She'd always wanted to be gorgeous and glamorous, and yet, when Rich said the words, they didn't sound right. Gorgeous wasn't enough. She wanted to be bright and clever *and* gorgeous.

"I guess we'd better get going," he whispered reluctantly against her hair. "We're already late for our reservation."

"Thanks for coming tonight," she said as he switched on the engine.

"I wouldn't have missed it for the world!" He smiled. "Tonight, Barri Gillette, you were a star!"

CHAPTER THIRTEEN

A week later, Barri and Rich met Joel at The Playhouse Theatre. They slipped into their seats just before the curtain went up on *Romeo and Juliet*. The crowd whispered in excited, hushed tones, and electricity charged the theatre.

The lights went down. The curtain lifted.

From the second the actors entered, Barri was swept away by the action. She couldn't take her eyes off the stage. When Ward McKenna, as Romeo, entered, the audience was transfixed. Even Joel's attention was center stage.

Melanie, as Juliet, was flawless. Fresh-faced, and clear-spoken, she was believable and entrancing. Her emotions flowed through the auditorium; Barri felt Juliet's accelerated heartbeat, her love, her anguish!

Barri's heart went out to her, and she forgot that Melanie was her best friend, a student at Fillmore. The girl onstage, with her hair braided away from her face, her long gowns diaphanous and flowing, *was* Juliet Capulet.

When Juliet spoke words of love to Romeo, everyone in the theater believed her. They held a special poignancy, a pain, that intensified the tragedy of these two timeless lovers.

The rest of the action was just as emotional—the sword fight incredible. Kurt and Robert, along with several other actors, parried and thrust, dancing and dodging as their swords glinted under the lights and sliced, hissing, through the air.

The fight looked so dangerous and believable that when Robert, as Mercutio, was slain and blood poured from his open wound, Barri gasped.

A few seconds later, Romeo, in swift, unthinking vengeance killed Tybalt, Juliet's cousin. Tears starred Barri's lashes. Romeo's pain was so pure—so perfect—when he realized what he'd done, that now he must be banished away from his Juliet forever!

And Juliet's suffering—so real—so intense! Melanie was perfect! Tears streamed down her face, her beautiful features twisted in agony at the prospect of never seeing Romeo alive again.

In Act five, when Juliet discovered Romeo's body, Barri grew cold. Melanie, her own expression lifeless, tears streaming from her eyes, took the dagger from Romeo and thrust the blade into her chest.

"No!" Barri whispered as Juliet fell.

When the final curtain dropped, the crowd was on its feet.

"Bravo! Excellent!" The audience exploded with shouts and whistles. "Encore! Encore!"

Barri dashed away her tears and clapped furiously as her friends reappeared to take their final bows.

Melanie and Ward were holding hands. To Barri their curtain call was the epitome of her own dreams. If only someday she could hold hands with her beloved and take a final bow to an auditorium filled with adoring fans clapping wildly!

Slowly the people in the audience began to collect their coats and purses before drifting toward the exits. Everyone seemed to be in good spirits, and the noise level was high. Barri knew that was a sure sign of a satisfied house.

"Come on," Joel whispered to Barri, "let's go backstage!"

Rich frowned. "I don't think we should—"

"Why not?" Joel tugged on Barri's arm, and Rich had no choice but to follow along, down the aisle to the stage and up the three short steps.

"Hey, you kids!" A beefy security guard caught up with them. "You can't go back there!"

Joel flashed his famous Amberson grin. "We're friends of Melanie Todd."

"I don't care if you're friends of President Bush. Out!"

"It's all right!" Melanie said, opening a door from the wings. "I thought you guys would be here."

"I've got strict orders," the guard insisted.

Barri ignored him. "You were fabulous, Melanie!" she said. "The greatest Juliet ever!"

"She's right," Joel agreed.

Melanie beamed and whispered to Barri, "Look, why don't you guys meet me at the Hamilton Hotel on Fifth? There's a cast party—"

"We can't!" Rich said.

"Sure we can," Joel said. "What room?"

"The Ben Franklin Room."

"We'll be there!" Joel replied, grinning at the security guard as they hurried outside.

Rich grabbed Joel's arm in the parking lot. "I don't know about you, but I'm not going to any cast party."

"Why not?"

"Why not? Because we aren't part of the cast, that's why!"

"But we were invited by a member of the cast," Joel pointed out. "Come on, Davies, Barri would love it."

Barri couldn't hide the excitement twinkling in her eyes. A cast party! With Ward McKenna! Maybe he'd have some friends there. Television people or agents or . . .

"Oh, all right," Rich grumbled, casting Barri a worried look.

"I'll drive!" Joel led them to an older-model Chrysler. "My mom's," he explained as he drove to the Hamilton Hotel.

Inside the grand old building Joel talked fast and furiously to several hotel personnel, and eventually they were allowed to enter a huge room with crystal chandeliers, silk-covered walls, and a thick burgundy carpet. Trays of hors d'oeuvres and a fountain of frothy orange punch filled a center table. Champagne was being offered to the adults.

"Isn't it great?" Melanie whispered as they walked past an ice sculpture of a graceful swan.

Barri's eyes moved around the room. Many of

the cast members were dressed in elegant clothes—silk gowns and tuxedos—jewels winking around throats and arms.

"Melanie, you were the greatest Juliet who ever lived."

"Or died," Joel added.

"Thanks." Melanie blushed and rolled her eyes. "I'm glad it turned out okay."

"Okay?" Joel said, "It went beyond *okay* to stupendous, enthralling, exquisite—"

"Oh, knock it off!" Melanie said, her cheeks turning from pink to scarlet as a wide, pleased grin crossed her features.

They sipped an exotic tropical punch and moved among the tables, talking with other members of the cast and crew.

Joel tugged at his collar, and Melanie's gaze roved restlessly over the crowd.

Barri knew whom she was looking for. "Where's Ward?" she asked.

"He hasn't shown up yet." Melanie's gaze skated from one knot of people to the next. "But I can't wait to see him," she whispered in Barri's ear. Melanie was so excited, she could barely speak. "After the performance he squeezed my hand and told me what a wonderful job I'd done. I nearly died and went to heaven!"

"So, he's coming to this party?"

"Oh, yes. He said he'd see me here. Oh, there he is now!"

Barri swung her gaze to the door, to see Ward enter the room. Every head turned his way. Melanie started to wave but stopped, her hand in mid-air, as she noticed the blonde with Ward. Jillian Donovan. Ward leaned over, whispered something in Jillian's ear, and she laughed gaily, tossing her head back.

Melanie gulped and her cheeks flamed.

Knowing Melanie was dying a thousand deaths, Barri turned to Rich. "You know," she said with forced cheerfulness. "Maybe you were right—maybe we shouldn't be here."

"Of course you should," Melanie insisted, but she couldn't hide the pain in her eyes.

Joel shrugged and shoved his hands into his pockets. "I don't know," he said, catching Barri's look, "we're a little underdressed."

"When has that ever mattered to you?" Melanie asked.

"Tonight. It, uh, matters tonight," Joel lied. "So, maybe we should go over to Prime-Time. This place is a little too highbrow for me."

"But it's the cast party. . . ." Melanie said miserably as she watched Ward circle Jillian in his arms.

"Its *D.U.L.L.*," Joel insisted, grabbing Melanie's hand. "Let's lose this crowd. Robert and Kurt aren't even here. We can go talk about the play over a huge pizza."

"Sure," Barri insisted, though she hated to leave the glittery party.

"I know what you're trying to do," Melanie sniffed.

"Good. Then you won't fight about it."

Twenty minutes later all the Thespians were

crowded around a huge taco pizza, and even
Geraldine ate a small piece, proclaiming it to be,
"not all that bad."

Melanie, though she put on a brave front,
seemed preoccupied.

"It's all my fault," she confided quietly to Barri.
"Why would a star like Ward McKenna fall for
me?"

"Oh, I don't know," Barri said with a grin.
"Maybe because you're beautiful, clever, and the
best Juliet anyone's ever seen in Merion or any-
where else."

"Do you really think so?" Melanie asked.

"Didn't I already say so? Weren't you listening?"

Melanie sighed. "I guess I just like hearing it."

"Of course you do. We all do. Tonight you
proved to the whole world, including Ward Mc-
Kenna, that you're going to be one of the greatest classical actresses ever to set foot center
stage!"

Belatedly Melanie grinned and eyed the remains
of the pizza. "Let's have another," she finally said,
getting into the party spirit.

"That's more like it!" Joel said. "How about a
sausage, pepperoni, and hamburger?"

Geraldine made a face. "Olive, mushroom, onion, and double cheese."

Joel and Geraldine squared off as they ordered.

Barri grinned and snuggled closer to Rich in the
booth. Things were back to normal at last!

* * *

"Barri?" Her mother called from the bottom of the stairs. "Telephone for you. Someone from a television station."

Barri dropped her brush and dashed from her room. She flew down the stairs and snatched the phone from her mother's hand. Could it be? Had she won the soap opera contest? She tingled all over. "Hello?" she said, unable to hide the breathless tone of her voice.

"Barri Gillette?"

"Yes."

"This is Trish Sanders. I'm an assistant producer of 'Tomorrow Is Another Day.' "

"Oh." Barri's knees went weak. She had to lean against the kitchen counter for support, and she knew her mother was watching her.

Celia Gillette's eyes met her daughter's and asked silently, *What's going on?*

Ms. Sanders continued, "We received your entry, and your reasons for wanting to audition for a small part on the show were great. You, along with twenty-four other entrants, have been chosen to try out."

"Really?" Barri squealed. "Really? I have?"

"Yes," Trish Sanders replied, laughing. "Can you come to New York on the twentieth to audition?"

"I wouldn't miss it for the world!" Barri wanted to scream and hoot and yell, but she forced her voice back into the calm zone. She was speaking with a producer, and she had to sound professional. But it was killing her!

She listened as Ms. Sanders described the audition process. Then, before the producer hung up, Barri couldn't help but gush, "This is just the greatest news! I *adore* 'Tomorrow Is Another Day'! My aunt plays Beth Merriweather on the show, and I can't believe I've got a chance to work with her!"

"Your aunt?"

"Yes, Aunt Laura. Laura Layton."

"Laura Layton is related to you?" Ms. Sanders voice had lost some of its animation.

Was the woman deaf? "Yes. She's my mom's sister."

"You're Laura's niece?" There was a pause, and Barri had the awful premonition that something was wrong. "Did you read the rules of the contest?"

"Yes—"

"Then you realize that anyone related to anyone who works on the show is automatically disqualified."

"Disqualified?" Barri whispered, her chest suddenly constricted. Her throat grew hot. "Disqualified." Her mother took a step closer.

"Barri?" Celia asked quietly.

Ms. Sanders voice was soft. "I'm sorry, Miss Gillette, but under the rules of the contest, you can't possibly audition for the part."

Barri's throat closed. Tears stung her eyes. "But you said—"

"I know, and I'm really sorry. But those are the rules."

Before she broke down altogether and made a fool of herself, Barri whispered, "I understand," and hung up. But she didn't understand. Just because she was Laura Layton's niece wasn't any reason to discriminate against her.

"Barri," her mother asked, her brows drawing together in worry, "what's wrong? What is it?"

"Oh, Mom," Barri wailed, wishing she could hold back her tears and failing miserably. "I had a chance to act on 'Tomorrow Is Another Day,' and I blew it!"

"How? What're you talking about?"

Sobbing wretchedly, Barri fell into her mother's arms and poured out her heart.

"Oh, honey, I'm sorry," her mother whispered when Barri had finally explained about the contest. "You should have talked to me about it."

"It was going to be a surprise," Barri replied, dabbing her eyes with a tissue and feeling as if her world were literally crumbling apart.

"There'll be other parts."

"But this would have been so perfect! When will I ever get a chance to work with Aunt Laura?"

Mrs. Gillette sighed. "You've got years ahead of you. You can't do everything at once."

Refusing to be consoled, Barri ran upstairs and flopped down on her bed. Her room was filled with mementos from her recent performance as Jamie Winston. Several reviews were pinned to her bulletin board, roses and carnations drooped in two vases, and the silver pumps and bag were on display on her dresser. She didn't care. The thrill of being Jamie Winston had faded, and she felt wretched.

As if understanding her blues, Felicia hopped

from the windowsill and jumped onto the bed. Barri barely noticed until the fat tabby crawled onto her stomach and curled into a contented ball. "You weigh a ton!" Barri muttered ungraciously, but patted Felicia's furry head anyway, listening as the cat began to purr loudly.

She was still lying on her bed, rebelling against studying her latest history assignment when the phone rang again.

"Who cares?" she said to Felicia.

"Hey, it's for you!" Jeff yelled at the top of his lungs.

"Okay, okay!" She gave the cat a nudge, and Felicia grudgingly hopped onto the floor. "I'll get it in Mom's room!"

As she picked up the receiver, she heard Jeff click off downstairs. "Hello?"

"Barri? It's Aunt Laura. I just heard the news."

Barri fell across her parents' bed and felt like crying all over again. "Isn't it just awful?"

"Yes and no."

"Yes and yes," Barri corrected.

"Well, I know this doesn't sound quite as exciting as being on the show, but I called to invite you and Melanie to come and visit me in New York sometime after the first of the year. I'll have a little more breathing room in my schedule then. We could go to a play, see the city, do some shopping or whatever you want to do."

"Really?" Barri's flagging spirits took flight. Manhattan with Aunt Laura and Melanie!

"Really!" Aunt Laura said, laughing. "It'll be my birthday present to you. What do you say?"

In all the excitement, Barri had scarcely given any thought to the fact that she was going to turn sixteen in just a few more weeks. "I can't wait!"

"Neither can I! Look, I've got to run, but I'll call you later with the details."

"Okay, but just one question," Barri said.

"Shoot."

Barri's eyes narrowed. "Did Mom put you up to this?"

"I'll never tell," Laura said with a throaty laugh and hung up.

Barri's feet barely touched the steps as she raced downstairs. Her mother and Jeff were in the kitchen at the table, struggling with Jeff's list of spelling words.

"*R-e-c-i-e-v-e.*" Jeff said.

"Remember *i* before *e* except—"

"Did you call Aunt Laura?" Barri demanded, her face splitting with a wide grin.

"I thought you could use a little cheering up," her mother admitted.

"For my birthday present, she invited Melanie and me to stay with her in New York."

"Isn't that wonderful!"

"*You're* wonderful!" Barri hugged her mom. "I just know this is going to be my big break!" Barri declared dreamily, already envisioning her future. She could meet actors, dancers, singers, producers, directors, theatre people, agents, movie moguls—the list went on and on. Sighing happily, she said, "I have a good feeling about this trip to

New York already. You know, I may just be *discovered*!"

"Give me a break," Jeff said, rolling his eyes.

"Maybe she will," Celia Gillette said with a knowing smile. Barri couldn't help grinning ear to ear. "And I thought my life was ruined!"

"Just remember, tomorrow *is* another day," her mother quipped, and even Jeff laughed.

Here's a look at what's ahead in *Barri, Take Two*, the second book in Fawcett's CENTER STAGE series for GIRLS ONLY.

Geraldine Horowitz came flying down the school hall, toward Barri and Melanie, jangling bracelets and waving scarves. Geraldine was the Thespians' main costumer and scenic designer, and she was flamboyant and full of energy. "I heard you're going to New York to see a taping of *Tomorrow Is Another Day*! You're so lucky!"

"I'm still waiting for the final word from my dad," Melanie moaned. "If he doesn't let me go I'll just die."

"He has to let you go," Barri said with confidence. "He just has to."

"Tell him that." Melanie heaved a huge sigh. "Last fall he was on an austerity kick. Now he thinks I don't spend enough time with my family."

Geraldine's blue eyes were filled with envy. "If she can't go, Barri, keep me in mind! I would l-o-v-e to meet some of those actors. They're scrumptious. Did you see this?" She dug inside her mammoth-sized black bag and pulled out a copy of *Hollywood Heart Throbs.*

Melanie groaned. "Another rag? What happened to *Teen Idols*? Geraldine, I swear, you're a disgrace to the acting community."

"Oh, come on. You've read teen magazines before," Barri reminded Melanie, looking over Geraldine's shoulder.

"But I would never buy one!" Melanie said with a sniff.

Geraldine snapped open the magazine, throwing an angry glance at Melanie who pretended not to notice. "It's bad enough Joel gets on my case all the time. I don't need you, too!"

"Okay, okay," Barri inserted quickly. "What were you going to show us?"

"This." She turned to the center story. Inside was a full cast picture of *Tomorrow Is Another Day.* The caption read: Newcomer to the soaps is sizzling hot! Meet Nick Castle. Port Michaels' latest teenage Mr. Right!

"Who is this guy?" Melanie asked.

"He's only been on the show a couple of times," Barri said. "He's Dr. Monahan's son from his first marriage."

"Second marriage," Geraldine corrected her. "Dr. Monahan's on his third already."

"Unbelievable," Melanie muttered, shaking her head. "But I'm not complaining," she added hastily, catching Barri's sideways glance. "I'd do just about anything to go! Even subscribe to *Hollywood Heart Throbs*, if I had to. Nothing's going to stop me. Nothing."

If Writing
Is an Artform,
Let
A FEW OF OUR AUTHORS
Paint a Picture
For You . . .

THE PORTRAITS SERIES